MAKING THE MOST OF IT

MAKING THE MOST OF IT

LISA FORREST

HODDER

To Jess
for the Great Seashell Party and many other things

A Hodder Book

Published in Australia and New Zealand in 2000
by Hodder Headline Australia Pty Limited
(A member of the Hodder Headline Group)
Level 22, 201 Kent Street, Sydney NSW 2000
Website: www.hha.com.au

National Library of Australia
Cataloguing-in-Publication data

Forrest, Lisa
Making the most of it.

ISBN 0 7336 0794 2.
I. Swimming – Juvenile fiction. I. Title.
A823.3

Text design and typesetting Egan-Reid Ltd
Author photo: David Ryrie
Printed in Australia by Griffin Press, Adelaide

CHAPTER ONE

NINA SAT FIFTH in the line-up of eight girls, unconscious of the nervous toe-tap her feet were performing. Usually, this part of the night—the wait from the marshalling call to the beginning of the race—seemed to take forever. But tonight Nina was glad of the chance it gave her to catch her breath and gather her thoughts.

What a disaster the night had been so far. As if making the final of the 100m Backstroke at the Commonwealth Games Selection Trials wasn't nerve-racking enough! Dad had been held up at work so they didn't get on the road until late. Then travelling through peak-hour traffic had been a true exercise in patience. Luckily, they had been aiming to get to the pool an hour early for a good warm-up or they would have missed the race entirely.

Nina was sure her face mirrored the look of relief she saw in the eyes of her coach, Jack, when she burst through the pool entrance. She flashed her finals card at the attendant who let her pass onto the pool deck.

'Traffic,' she said as she dumped her bag at Jack's feet, tore off her clothes and grabbed her cap and goggles.

'Plenty of time,' her coach replied as he walked her to the pool's edge. 'Swim two or three hundred, nice and steady, we'll do a couple of sprints and you'll be ready to go.'

Nina knew that with fifteen minutes of warm-up time remaining she did not have plenty of time. But she wasn't about to state the obvious. Anyway, she'd forgotten about it moments later when she dived in.

1

From the time she was a little girl, the water had rolled itself around her like a soft protective film, soothed her jagged movements and turned her normal clumsiness into the most exquisite and elegant of gestures. Tonight it did all that and more. The weightlessness she felt as she skimmed through the water was almost frightening. She skipped like the smoothest stone across a glassy lake, hardly rippling the surface. This had been happening for a few days now. She hadn't told anyone. She didn't dare. Not even her father. She didn't want to risk speaking about it in case it took away the magic. But it was all so effortless it made her giddy.

Fifteen minutes flew by and she was running again, this time to the change rooms to squeeze herself into her racing swimmers. Then it was off to the marshalling area, a small room under the grandstand. The 100m Backstroke Final was the first event of the Commonwealth Games Selection Trials. There hadn't been time to talk race tactics with Jack. There hadn't been time to get good luck wishes from her mum and dad. Suddenly she thought of her lucky swimming cap—her Aquanauts Club cap that she had worn in the last eight backstroke races and swum best times in every one. Where was it? She pulled out the entire contents of her bag before finding it in one of the inside pockets. She laughed to herself and silently thanked her mother, who was surely responsible for putting it there, dried, powdered and ready to wear.

As the race marshal entered the room and called the swimmers, Nina stuck her head around the doorway and quickly scanned the grandstand for her parents. She found Jack sitting with some of the other squad members. She knew her mother and father would be in that general vicinity, but where?

'Nina Hallet, lane five,' called the marshal.

'Here,' called Nina, 'be there in one minute.' Just then she spotted him. She knew she didn't have much time; she would have to go the next time the marshal called. 'Come on,

Daddy-o,' she whispered, willing him to look down to the pool deck and see her head poking around the doorway. As if the magic force that propelled her through the pool was still with her, he turned at that moment and saw her there. Blowing Nina a kiss, he dragged his wife's attention away from the concentrated conversation she was having with Jill Harrigan's mother, and pointed to Nina. Her mum gave her a big wave and Nina smiled back at them both. Now she could concentrate.

The marshalling area—or ready room—was a small, low-ceilinged room of blond brick and cement situated on the pool deck level. A glass wall separated the room's inhabitants from the pool itself and gave them a narrow glimpse of what was going on outside. At any other time during the evening it was the marshalling area for, at most, two races. But because this was the beginning of the night, it was operating as a sort of general holding area for swimmers and officials alike. Concentration was almost impossible.

Nina could hear Jack's words in her head. 'Sit down, conserve your energy,' but she ignored them. 'Just for a moment,' she told herself. Rather than sapping her energy, she found the busy mood of the room somehow heightened her own consciousness. The air became tangible, percolating deliciously through her body until she broke out in goosebumps.

She became conscious of a couple of officials trying to get her attention. They were representatives of her own swimming club, the Aquanauts, and Nina gave them a nod. Mrs Dean, the president of the club, discreetly gave a quick flash of her hand, which had the index and middle fingers crossed for good luck.

There were about forty officials getting last-minute instructions and taking care of general business. They would spend the night watching starts, turns, finishes and strokes to ensure they were all executed within the rules of the sport. Nina found it somehow reassuring that, as a group, the officials seemed to be in as much of a hurry as she was for the night to begin. She couldn't wait to get in the water and race.

'Just a lot of adrenaline flowing through your system, ninja-girl,' she thought, using her father's pet name for her. The use of the nickname surprised her. It wasn't her favourite. She thought it was kind of daggy. But tonight it was strangely comforting. 'Bit nervous are we?' she teased. 'Gotta keep that under control.'

She looked over to the row of women she was meant to join. Hers was the fifth chair in the line. It was a basic arrangement that meant she would swim the final from lane five, having qualified with the second fastest time in the heats that had been swum that morning. It was not a position she was used to competing from. At least, not in open competition. Swimming against other fourteen-year-olds, she usually finished in the top three. But at the Open Nationals, where girls were up to ten years older, she was used to contesting the race from the outside lanes—one or eight. Up to this point in her athletic 'career' no one would have said that Nina Hallet was a major threat to the big guns.

But that had all changed that morning in the heats. Nina had been beating her own best times consistently that summer. She was pretty confident she could improve again, but whether that would put her among the fastest eight to go through to the final was impossible to predict.

Nina knew that as she stood behind the blocks that morning, ready for the first of four heats. The grandstands were empty but for the swimmers, coaches and parents involved specifically in the heats. There were no other spectators. Atmosphere was non-existent. An embarrassed groan had escaped from Nina when, just before she jumped into the water to start the race, her father had yelled, 'Go ninja-girl!' It had echoed countless times in the great cavernous dome that housed the competition and diving pools.

From the moment the gun had released the swimmers from their crouched starting positions, Nina had led the field. When she won the heat she had swum two seconds faster than she had ever swum before. She had also swum the second fastest time ever by an Australian. Only Inga Holder had swum faster, and she was in one of the heats still to come. In one moment, Nina had broken the concentration of every other girl in that event. The hierarchy that existed in the backstroke events was suddenly under threat. Rather than thinking about their own performance, three questions now dominated the thoughts of the rest of the competitors. Who was this girl? Where did she come from? Can I swim as fast as her?

Nina was oblivious to this and to the new status she held as she sat in her chair. She was only conscious that she didn't know any of them. None of these girls raised so much as a smile. Inga Holder—the fastest qualifier and undisputed queen of Australian swimming—made Nina wait until she decided, somewhat reluctantly, to remove her belongings from the chair Nina was supposed to sit in. Inga was in lane four. She had been the number one sprint-backstroker for Australia since her inclusion in the Olympic Games team almost two years ago. She was also beautiful. At twenty years of age, tall, blonde and lean, she was as stunning as any supermodel, and sponsors fought for the right to have her endorse their products. She was also something of a mystery because she was good over just the one distance—one hundred metres of backstroke. She didn't bother swimming anything else. So her presence seemed somehow royal. She would arrive. Charm the few lucky enough to find themselves in her orbit. Win her race, effortlessly. Then graciously accept her medal and take her leave. She managed to give the impression that not only

5

was she unattainable but that the race she deigned to compete in was out of the reach of mere mortals.

Jebby Cross, the two hundred-metre champion, was on the other side of Nina in lane six. Nina realised that while she was sitting next to one of her heroes, she had now swum faster than the other girl ever had over the shorter distance. Jebby was a couple of years older than Inga, but a contemporary in terms of experience.

Over in lane three, Georgia Chow made up the reigning Australian backstroke troika. Georgia occasionally beat Inga and Jebby over both distances but most often she was a consistent third. With only two swimmers selected per event to compete at the Commonwealth Games, Nina knew Inga and Jebby were the major threat to her chances of making the team. They were quite capable of halting her assault on their positions before it even began.

Jack had talked about these three girls many times to Nina. In his estimation, this was the best chance Nina would have to make the team. All three girls had been travelling heavily over the past year and, by his calculations, had not had a consistent period of hard training for quite a while. So, while their race experience was greater than Nina's, their stamina might not be.

Nina's private summation of her rivals was interrupted when she sensed Inga looking at her. Embarrassed that the other girl might have somehow read her mind, she turned to find her rival looking at her legs, which Nina now noticed were uncontrollably bouncing up and down on the spot.

'Must you do that?' Inga demanded loudly.

'Sorry,' replied Nina genuinely. 'Actually, I didn't realise . . .' But the rest of her admission was drowned out by an exasperated sigh from the other girl. Inga was not about to engage in meaningless chatter.

For a moment Nina's heart raced. How could she have

been so stupid to think Inga Holder was about to talk to her? Even worse, she seemed to have genuinely annoyed her. How could she have been such a drip? She would have a long way to go now if she were to prove herself vaguely sophisticated enough to talk to Inga. And the others. She was sure they had all heard the exchange. And after swimming so well this morning, showing that maybe she was good enough to be in their league! She was always doing things like that, saying the wrong thing, tripping over in front of someone.

Nina looked at Inga, wondering if she should apologise. But the other girl had draped a towel over her head and was leaning down, elbows on knees. Something about the woman's posture made Nina pause. What was that she had been thinking? To have annoyed Inga Holder. Had something as simple as another girl's nervous fidgeting annoyed this champion? Nina's brain seemed to shift and fall into a place of much greater understanding.

Suddenly all the pedestals had been removed. Not just Inga Holder but every other girl in the race was within Nina's grasp tonight. She couldn't wait to tell her dad about her discovery. He would get a laugh. It wasn't so long ago that he was coming to the marshalling area with her because she was too shy to go alone. The big question now was should she deliberately start her annoying toe-tap again and really drive her opponent around the twist? Nina wondered if it fell within the conduct of being 'a good sport'.

'I'll do it just for a moment, to see how she reacts,' thought Nina. Pretending to look in the opposite direction she re-sumed, ever so innocently, the offending movement. Out of the corner of her eye she saw Inga's head whip around to the source of the disturbance. Failing to get Nina's attention a second time, Inga managed to contain her obvious agitation and say nothing.

Nina's moment of glee was cut short when the officials

began to move, signalling the start of the evening. Soon the only official left was the Starter. After he had given them their starting instructions, the obligatory strains of motivating music began and the finalists for the first race of the evening, the 100m Backstroke for Women, were led out of the room to the starting end of the pool.

Nina had never felt more alive. The grandstands were full of people. Even the Open National Championships that Nina had competed at was not as crowded as these Commonwealth Games Selection Trials. She had never experienced the physical power that came from the roar of a large group of people. Not even listening to her favourite music full-blast or watching a movie in full stereo sound at the cinema had ever shaken her body with as much force.

As she marched along the poolside she searched again for her mother and father. They were on their feet cheering and waving along with most of the other people from her squad. She felt a little embarrassed and wished they would sit down. Should she wave back? None of the other finalists were waving. Nina decided to just give them a big smile and hoped they could see it.

Just then she saw Jack. He was a little removed from the rest of the team, on the stairs between two sections of seating. Standing with his legs apart, he had one arm across his chest and the other resting on the crossed arm, supporting his chin. He was absolutely still. Nina knew that stance; it usually accompanied her toughest training sets. His immovable position would contrast with her racing heart as she pushed her fatigued arms and legs further and faster. And it most often came with steady, reassuring words that encouraged her to keep going, keeping at bay the voice in her own head that was screaming for respite.

Nina almost tripped the swimmers walking behind her as his focus on her brought her to a standstill.

'What the bloody hell are you doing?' hissed Jebby Cross as she swerved to avoid Nina, alerting the other swimmers to the potential danger.

'Sorry,' Nina automatically apologised.

But when Nina resumed her place in the line-up it was with a new sense of purpose. As they were led behind the starting blocks and introduced individually to the crowd, she found the distractions that had entertained her earlier were now in the background. The noise of the crowd, the other swimmers, her parents, they were all beyond the invisible wall that surrounded Nina the moment her concentration had been employed. Jack's gaze had bored through the artifice and reminded her of the hours of pain and determination it had taken for her to get here. As she stood waiting for the signal that would allow her to get into the pool, she concentrated on the long, narrow expanse of water that was her domain. Years of training converged to make this moment. She had never felt more powerful.

The okay was given and in she went. Let the others play their games, enter later, whatever. They could not avoid her. And there was that feeling again, that effortlessness.

A whistle brought them all back to the wall, 'take your mark' curled them into position and the Starter's gun sprung them into action. Nina's powerful underwater dolphin kick brought her to the surface in line with Inga, Jebby and Georgia. She often struggled to wind herself up in the first twenty-five metres of the sprint, but tonight she managed a good grip of the water without letting Inga make any headway at all.

'Wow,' thought Nina, 'that's what we want.' Inga was noted for flying starts that left the rest of the field trying to catch her. 'Better take it steady.' She reminded herself of Jack's constant warning to hold back, just a little, so she would have some energy left for the second half of the race.

Nina's turns were her strong point. She waited until just before the end of the first fifty metres to accelerate. Her feet landed on the wall just behind Inga's, but ahead of the other girls. When she had pulled out of her turn she was half a body length ahead of the field.

'Yes,' she said continuing the silent dialogue that had got her this far, 'now you go.' She concentrated on employing her big kick through the third twenty-five metres and hoped she wouldn't run out of puff by the end. Inga seemed to be struggling. 'Better watch out for Jebby Cross,' Nina warned herself, but no one seemed to be gaining. Moving into the last twenty-five metres, Nina's body was struggling to obey her commands. Everything burned. Every stroke felt laboured. The false start rope went by. The backstroke flags finally appeared. Four more strokes and it would all be over. Nina threw all the force she could muster into her final lunge at the wall and hit it ahead of the seven other swimmers.

A split-second later Jebby Cross, Inga Holder then Georgia Chow, in that order, joined Nina at the finish line. As Nina lurched for the lane rope to support her heaving body, her head seemed to spin. She was conscious of the crowd roaring. She thought she heard the pool announcer say something like 'the first upset of the night'. Suddenly, she panicked. 'Did I miss someone?' she asked herself. Was there someone who had surprised the spectators from an outside lane? Had she just made the most basic mistake—ignored anyone other than those closest to her? Jack would be furious at her stupidity.

'Check the scoreboard.' A voice of reason seemed to come from nowhere. She looked to the end of the pool. The swimmer in lane five had definitely won. 'That's me,' she noted, frustrated at the way she had to painstakingly weld the most rudimentary thoughts together. And then it registered. *She* was the upset.

'Mum and Dad,' Nina's eyes flew to the grandstand. She

found them jumping up and down, hugging one another and fielding congratulatory handshakes from everyone around them. It was then that she felt her first surge of joy. 'Oh' was the only sound she could make. When her father looked down at his daughter again he was delighted to find he had her attention. He raised both hands above his head and applauded her efforts. Her mother waved madly, occasionally stopping to look to the ground and wipe her face. The gesture seemed odd until Nina realised her mother was wiping away tears.

She became conscious of the other competitors. They swam over to shake her hand, say congratulations. Girls she had hardly spoken to before. Inga Holder gave her hand a limp shake and moved across the lanes out of the water. Jebby Cross slapped her on the back and said 'good girl' before getting out.

Nina followed the others, moving to the ladder at the side of the pool. As she lifted herself out of the water, the stadium erupted again, although it took her a moment to comprehend that the crowd was still focused on her. She automatically lifted her arm in acknowledgment. Her action surprised her as much as the cheering. 'Poser,' she laughed to herself.

Her action brought with it the flash of what seemed like a million lights. A wall of photographers had appeared in front of her, amassed behind a straining barricade. 'They must have been there before,' she reasoned, but she hadn't noticed them. Not sure whether to stand there and hold up the rest of the evening's proceedings, she looked around for some guidance. But the photographers demanded her attention.

'Nina, this way!'

'Over here, Nina!'

'Wave to the crowd, Nina!'

'Give us a big smile, love!'

She couldn't keep up with the commands. She wondered if she was doing it right.

Gradually she became aware of a more familiar chant rising above the whirring cameras. She looked up to see Jack hanging over the railing of the grandstand, waving his arms at her. Her friends Jake Watson, Tom Hoch and Angel Murphy flanked him. Jake, who prided himself on being something of a rapper, was bouncing around rapping her story to anyone who would listen. The other three were keeping the beat with the constant refrain, 'Nina Hallet is the girl, yeah, yeah, yeah, champion of our world, yeah, yeah, yeah'.

The sight of her portly coach punching the air to the beat as he sung away with the others was so incongruous that Nina forgot her self-consciousness in front of the cameras and fell about in delighted laughter. The immediate crowd understood the basic chant and joined in, much to Nina's embarrassment. When she shook her head and drew her hand horizontally in front of her throat to indicate 'cut', they ignored her. And when she threw up both her arms in mock exasperation, the photographers had a series of photos that would be on the front page of every newspaper around the country the next day.

Eventually an official saved Nina from further embarrassment by reminding her of the medal presentation. She applauded her friends' spontaneous performance and followed the man as he briskly led her under the grandstand to another room. In stark contrast to the noisy revelry that was going on outside, the room was quiet and almost empty. Only Jebby Cross and Inga Holder remained in the small space. As second and third place-getters they would also be collecting medals. They were already dressed.

'You've got a few minutes,' he told Nina.

Neither of the girls said anything to Nina as she dragged her tracksuit from her bag and pulled it on over her swimmers. Within a few minutes she was dressed. She stole a glance at the other two. Inga was looking into a small mirror, applying mascara. Jebby was combing her hair. Neither of them looked as though, only a few minutes before, they had been exhausting themselves trying to win a swimming race.

Inga was immaculate. Even in her pale blue and yellow club tracksuit she looked glamorous. She had parted her long blonde hair to one side and combed it flat to her head, pulling it together with a clip at the nape of her neck. She had applied dark smudges to the corner of her eyes and added a few strokes of mascara which, Nina noticed, further highlighted her already huge eyes. Jebby's hair, by contrast, was short and gave her a sort of pixie-like appearance. She reminded Nina of pictures she had seen of Jean Seberg, the film actress and activist, who was one of her mother's favourites. Jebby had applied a much heavier line to her eyes, which made her look tousled and hip compared to Inga's cool elegance.

Nina looked down at her own arrangement. She was always thankful she had joined a club that at least had the sense to use black and red as club colours rather than some of the other hideous combinations that were seen around the pool. She had made sure her mother had purchased a tracksuit that was a few sizes too big so that it hung low on her hips and draped onto the ground. Nina had convinced her mother that the pants needed a small zipper on the outside of each leg, which she always left open so that the base of her pants fanned around her trainers onto the floor. Her red Aquanauts T-shirt completed her ensemble. She was usually pretty happy with the way she looked, but next to the older girls she felt unsophisticated. She hadn't thought about make-up, although that wasn't unusual. She looked in her bag hoping a comb had found its way in there. But she would have been astonished to discover one. She was often in trouble at home for not combing her hair. She flipped her head over and ran her fingers roughly through her dark ringlets, shaking the curls loose. That would have to do.

Ceremonial music suddenly burst through the speakers at

such levels that audience and athletes alike automatically pressed their hands to their ears to shield them from the assault. By the time the volume had been adjusted, the girls had been ushered out of the room and were marching along the pool concourse. But the shock of the musical blast had at least broken the ice and Nina was able to share a surprised giggle with the other two girls as they made their way toward the presentation dais.

When they finally got to the end of the pool, Nina stood behind the number one dais, flanked by the women who only moments before had been her heroes and surrounded by two long grandstands full of people cheering and calling her name. When the pool announcer said: 'The winner of the 100m Backstroke for Women,' Nina was ready to launch herself up onto the number one spot. But when he added, 'With a new Commonwealth and Australian record,' she hesitated.

'It must be a mistake,' she thought. The pool started spinning again. In the excitement of winning she had forgotten to look at the time she had swum. Could it have been that fast? She didn't know what to do. She looked to the crowd. Found her mother and father, Jack, her friends. They were waving and shouting. None of them seemed to think it was a mistake. She looked at the girls either side of her. No protest from either of them. She heard Jebby Cross in her ear, 'Up you go'. Nina didn't think she could move. Jebby put her hand on Nina's back and gave her a gentle push. It propelled her body into action although her mind took a little longer to catch up. The pool stopped spinning. She was on top of the dais. She had come first. She had broken records. Nina thought she would burst. She gave a wave to the crowd, a smile to the people she knew. Bent down and felt the ribbon as it was placed around her neck, the weight of the gold medal as she stood up. She had surprised everyone, including herself.

And she couldn't wait to do it again.

CHAPTER TWO

NINA FOLLOWED THE two students ahead of her along the overgrown short cut to the main school grounds. The boys in front were laughing loudly and not aware of Nina's presence until a branch they pushed past flew back into her face.

'Ooww!' she exclaimed automatically.

The perfunctory 'sorry' was shot back with hardly a glance. But something made one of the boys stop and look again. Nina could barely see the boys through the tears that were stinging her eyes but she knew they were moving back toward her.

'Hey, aren't you that girl, you know, from the weekend?' He turned to his friend. 'The papers said she went to our school.' And to Nina, 'It's you, isn't it?' Nina managed to get in a nod before he continued, 'I forget your name though. What's your name again?'

'Nina.'

'Yeah, Nina that's right, Nina Hallet.' To his friend he went on, 'she got in the Commonwealth Games team on the weekend.' And to Nina, 'What do you swim again?'

'Umm, backstroke,' she replied, wiping her eyes. The stinging had subsided and she could see that he was older than she was.

'Yeah, backstroke, that's right. She won them both,' he said to his friend. 'Both the backstroke races. No one had heard of her before that.'

Another group of kids came along the bushy path. The boy

shouted to the new group, 'Hey, Jase, it's that girl from the weekend, Nina Hallet.'

Nina didn't know who Jase was. She didn't know any of them. All she knew was that between the overgrown bushes and the converging students she was beginning to wish she hadn't taken the short cut. The boy called Jase led a group of four more boys. He leant back as he looked at her.

'That was way cool, what you did on the weekend. Way cool.'

'Thanks.' She looked at the group of boys smiling at her. She smiled back, not knowing what else to do or say. Nina didn't know if the surrounding bushes were making her a little paranoid but the boys did seem to be looking at her strangely. There was admiration, definitely. But there was something else as well. A sort of acceptance. She had been given some new status that made her separate from anyone else.

She could hear more students coming along the path. She didn't want to seem ungrateful but she didn't want anyone else inspecting her.

'We'd better go, don't you think?' With the silence broken there was an embarrassed laugh from the boys. They all hung back letting her go first. At the last minute the original of-fender made a move.

'Wait, let me,' he offered as he dashed ahead of her, holding the branches apart for Nina to walk through.

'Thank you.' Nina looked at the boy and nodded to include all the others. 'See you.'

The bell was ringing as she made her way into the quadrangle. Every morning the seven hundred students that made up Harper High amassed in the large square for roll call and assembly. Harper was a school typical of many built in the seventies. All natural brick, exposed concrete and steel girders of varying colours. As she moved into the area she wondered what was on the bulletin board on the other side of the quadrangle that had so many students milling around it. Nina had missed school the week before to compete at the selection trials. She hoped it wasn't something she had to know about for today. Although the bell was ringing the students didn't seem to be in a rush to move away from the board.

Nina began jogging across the square, dodging lines of students. As she moved she mentally berated herself. She had been distracted last week with the trials. Still, she should have been more thorough finding out about the work she would miss; what would need to be prepared for this week. She hoped it wasn't something important. Her mother would be cross if she found out. And she would find out. Nina always supposed it was her mother's natural inclination toward curiosity that allowed her to find out so much about everything. That, and her ability to make anyone she was talking to feel totally at ease, thereby divulging all sorts of information. Nina broke into a sweat that wasn't only due to her jogging.

As she reached the edge of the group, Mrs Bevan, one of the social science teachers, was moving to disperse the small crowd.

'Come on, you can look at that later.'

Unable to see through the group, Nina turned to go back to her line. But snatches of sentences she couldn't help overhearing made her turn back around. She found a see of faces staring at her, some familiar, some not.

'Nina!' shrieked Alice Hinkel. 'Oh my God, Nina. Can you believe it? What was it like? Oh my God, isn't it exciting?'

Nina had heard, rather than seen, Alice first. Unusual, because Alice was a girl difficult to miss in size and manner. Luckily, Nina caught her moving out of the corner of her eye, giving her a split second to anticipate Alice's bear hug. Moving sideways she avoided being completely engulfed by Alice's fleshy arms and sizeable chest. It wasn't that Nina didn't like

Alice. On the contrary, she admired Alice's ability to ignore the school Nazis that tried to determine how you should look, what you should wear and how you should behave. No, Nina's sideways move merely enabled her to breathe during what she knew would be a hearty congratulatory hug.

Alice's unabashed enthusiasm for Nina's achievements led others to join in, making it even harder for Mrs Bevan to be effective.

'C'mon guys, you can do this later. I need everyone to move into their House lines. Away you go. You can talk to Nina later.' As she spoke, Mrs Bevan pushed through the group until she reached Nina.

'Come on, Alice.' Mrs Bevan exaggerated the words this time. 'Give the girl a chance to breathe.'

Alice giggled. 'Oh, Mrs. Bevan. I wasn't hugging her that hard. Was I, Nina?'

Nina pretended to pant heavily. 'No,' she struggled to breathe, 'Alice,' still struggling, 'no,' panting again, 'harm,' starting to get her breath back, 'done!' She couldn't keep a straight face and Alice, Nina and Mrs Bevan started giggling.

'Oh, Nina,' Alice screeched, still laughing.

'Off to your line, Alice. And everyone else, too. Mr Jenkins is addressing assembly this morning and we have already held it up.'

As Nina turned to follow Alice, Mrs Bevan called her back. 'Not you, Nina.'

Just then Nina heard her name called over the loud-speaker. 'Nina Hallet to the front of assembly, please. Would Nina Hallet come to the front of assembly.'

Nina looked at Mrs Bevan for an explanation.

'You don't think you do something like that on the weekend and come back to school as if nothing has happened? Congratulations, young lady, you've caused quite a stir!'

She followed Mrs Bevan with her eyes as the teacher

walked away. She liked Mrs Bevan. She had never been taught by her but had heard only good things about her. Nina was sure she was the kind of teacher who would have forgiven her escaping down the corridor that stretched in front of her and out the side gates to hide in the shop across the road until assembly was over. She had never done it before but she'd heard other kids talking about it. It couldn't be that hard. It had to be better than being hauled up in front of the assembly. Nina looked the other way to see who was watching. As she did, her eye caught the bulletin board and she saw what the others had been looking at.

Someone had covered it in press clippings from the weekend's newspapers, all heralding her efforts. The papers had gone crazy when she had beaten Inga Holder in the 100m but they had gone into overdrive when she added the 200m to her winning achievements. And it was all there in front of her. Across the top of the board was a green cardboard banner with gold letters that read: 'Congratulations Nina Hallet Year 9!'

Once again, the announcement came over the loud speaker. 'Nina Hallet would you please come to the front of the assembly. Nina Hallet to the front of the assembly, please.'

It was the unmistakable voice of Mr Jenkins, the school principal. Did she dare ignore the principal and flee? She heard a familiar voice behind her.

'Well, if it isn't the girl herself.'

Shan Wilcox. Pretty much the coolest girl in Year 9. Behind her was Ruby Taylor, the second coolest.

Too late to run, Nina thought to herself.

'Hi Shan, hi Ruby.'

Nina had greeted these girls many times, usually without response. But today their eyes were fixed on her. Nina found herself being reassessed, again. This time not as favourably. She didn't know how to take the conversation further. Few people did with Shan. She made sure she always had the upper hand.

LISA FORREST

'Well? You'd better get up there, girlfriend, they're calling your name.'

Nina nodded, only to turn and see the bulletin board again. Oh no, did they think she had been standing there reading about herself? She put her head down and headed toward the podium at the front of the assembly. She would worry about it later. Anyway, she reminded herself, Shan had used the word 'girlfriend'. Nina's mother hated that expression.

'So American,' she always said, 'can't you find an expression of your own?' But Shan Wilcox had called her 'girlfriend'. What a weird day it was and it was only beginning.

Mr Jenkins was waiting on the podium when she got there. He walked toward her, long lanky strides, smiling his very toothy grin, his right hand outstretched. Nina had just begun to proffer her own hand when he grabbed it, shaking it so rapidly she thought he would pull her arm out of its socket.

'We're very proud, Nina. Very proud. We are just so proud. A marvellous effort! Wasn't it, Mrs Ridge? Marvellous! Aren't we proud?'

Mrs Ridge was the school's deputy principal and the regular leader at morning assembly. She was also Nina's maths teacher.

'Yes, Mr Jenkins, marvellous it is. Although I don't know what we are going to do about all the school she's going to miss. When do you leave us, Nina?'

'End of the week, Mrs Ridge.'

'And for how long?'

'About eight weeks.'

'Eight weeks! My goodness!'

Nina hoped she wasn't going to make too much of it. She had been silently mortified when, after the team had been selected on Sunday night, one of the parents had raced up to her mother and father looking for some back-up in securing a tutor for the few school-age swimmers while they were away.

Luckily her parents had not been interested. Whether it was faith in Nina's ability to make up the lost time when she returned or just that they were new to this and had no intention of rocking the boat for Nina, she wasn't sure. She was just grateful they had rejected the proposal.

Thankfully Mr Jenkins, who had a look in his eyes not unlike the boys Nina had encountered earlier, paid little attention to Mrs Ridge's streak of practicality. 'Nonsense, Mrs Ridge. There are plenty of people willing to help her catch up on a few weeks of missed school for such an opportunity. Don't you worry about that, Nina.'

When Mrs Ridge finished the general housekeeping notes, she handed the microphone over to Mr Jenkins.

'Men and women of Harper.' His opening address had always made Nina giggle.

'I won't take up much of your time. As you probably know by now, one of our students acquitted herself in the most outstanding manner over the weekend. I'm sure many of you had never heard of Nina Hallet, but after swimming faster than anyone else in her backstroke races on the weekend, the whole country now knows who she is. So I guess we had all better catch up. Nina, come forward, please.'

Mr Jenkins turned and motioned for her to come and stand next to him. She went halfway.

'Come on, Nina, everyone wants to see you.' And to the assembly, 'No wonder no one ever noticed her before.' There was a general laugh from the students that seemed to reverberate around the quadrangle. Nina smiled at the sea of people, not sure what else to do. When she was standing next to Mr Jenkins he continued.

'Representing our great country is the highest accolade anyone can achieve or have bestowed upon them. I know you will want to help me congratulate Nina Hallet for her success on the weekend. And wish her the very best for the

Commonwealth Games next month.' With that he gave the microphone back to Mrs Ridge and began clapping. The rest of the school followed suit.

The sea of wildly applauding, cheering people kept Nina rooted to the spot. She had spent the last four days in front of cheering crowds but she was still getting used to it. Of course she was grateful. But it was weird. She was being treated to a totally new perspective of the world. Nina had always thought of herself as just one of the crowd. And while not exactly expendable, she always felt like she was way out on the edge looking in. Suddenly, everyone was looking at her. She had their attention but she wasn't sure that she wanted it.

Nina nodded to the crowd, saying thank you to them all, hoping she'd be allowed to leave, but her action brought on another round of applause. She looked at Mr Jenkins to help her out but he just grabbed her hand and started shaking it, very vigorously, again. She turned and appealed to Mrs Ridge who either read her thoughts or decided the whole thing had gone on long enough. She moved to the front of the podium.

'Thank you Mr Jenkins, students. I am sure you will all get a chance to congratulate Nina individually over the next few days. It's time to get to first period. We've eaten into ten minutes of that time already. Thank you, school. Off you go.'

The crowd dispersed. Nina gathered her utility bag from the back of the podium. Mr Jenkins appeared by her side. 'Cricket was my sport you know, Nina.'

'Oh, really, Mr Jenkins?'

'Yeah. Bowler. Fast. Well, pretty fast. Not as fast as Lillee and Thompson though.' He looked off toward the emptying quadrangle. 'Played for New South Wales. Couple of Shield Games. Didn't make it any further, though.'

He paused. Nina followed his gaze into the quadrangle but couldn't see anything that might have caught his attention. What do I say? she thought.

'That's still pretty good, Mr Jenkins, you know. Some people never do that.' Including herself, she thought. She'd never represented New South Wales. Now she was representing Australia.

He shook off his thoughts. 'Anyway, don't worry about, you know, what Mrs Ridge said. Plenty of time for school. Just make the most of your trip. The Commonwealth Games are in Manchester, aren't they?'

Nina nodded. 'A training camp first, in Paris. Then the Games. And then the World Championships in Los Angeles, if I get selected. Depends on how I swim in Manchester.'

'Well, remember to enjoy yourself. It might never happen again, you know.' He turned and was making his way back toward his office when he yelled back at her, 'And come and see me if you need anything.'

'Thank you,' she yelled back. Did I say the right thing? she thought. She had not been prepared for her school principal to make what seemed to be a sort of confession. What do you say to something like that? Gee, that's too bad, Mr Jenkins! She would have to ask her parents.

The rest of the class were pretty much seated when Nina got to science. Mrs Johnson, their science teacher, was yet to arrive so conversation was flying around the room. Nina put her head down and tried to slip through the door and to her desk, without bringing attention to herself. She was unsuccessful.

'Nina, I've saved you a seat over here.' It was Alice.

'I always sit here, Alice.' Nina was about to give a 'thanks-for-announcing-my-arrival' look but the other girl's face was so full of disappointment she didn't have the heart.

'But we've got so much to ask you about,' Alice wailed.

'Yeah, like what's Dominic Ray really like, Nina?' Shan Wilcox from the back of the classroom. 'Or doesn't he waste his time with the baby of the team.' Although Shan had picked up on a term used by the papers to describe Nina's swimming experience, she had loaded it with a little more meaning.

'He seemed nice, Shan.'

'You talked to him?' Shan challenged.

'Yes, I talked to him.' She smiled, firmly, at the other girl. She prayed she wasn't blushing. Technically, Nina was telling the truth. Dominic Ray, 200m Individual Medley world record holder and *Hip Magazine*'s reigning 'Coolest Catch of the Year', had been very nice to her. What she didn't tell Shan was that, still charged with the excitement of winning on that first night, she was making her way out of the pool to meet her mum and dad. In her hurry she had cut a corner too finely and tripped over one of the freestanding sponsor billboards. She would have done herself much worse damage if she hadn't fallen, literally, into the arms of Dominic Ray.

'Hey! What's going on!' Nina had heard.

'Ugh, oh goodness, I'm so sorry,' she had said before she had recovered her balance. Or realised who she was speaking too. When she looked up she couldn't believe it. She was sure her face had resembled a clown at sideshow alley.

'Wow, take it easy!' He shook the arm that had taken most of her weight. While he checked that he wasn't injured himself he kept talking to her. 'Are you hurt?'

She shook her head, too stunned to do anything more. When he didn't hear a reply he looked at her and was about to ask again when he caught himself.

'Oh, it's you.'

She nodded.

'You did a good job tonight. Congratulations.' He held out his hand to introduce himself. 'I'm Dominic.'

Nina tried to say something: I'm not hurt; thanks; I know who you are; anything. But nothing would come out. All she knew was that she had almost done permanent damage to every girl's idol and she couldn't even say sorry. She wished the pavement would swallow her whole. She shook his hand.

'Are you okay?' He tried again.

She nodded. 'Embarrassed,' she managed to squeeze out in a voice she didn't recognise. She backed away from him. She almost fell over the billboard again but she pulled herself up in time. He smiled ever so sweetly at her as she made her way past him.

'Take care of yourself, Nina,' she heard him say, 'we need you on that team.'

As she walked away, more carefully this time, she was pleased he couldn't see the look of triumph on her face. She had made the Commonwealth Games team, sure. But even better than that, Dominic Ray knew who she was.

Shan's voice brought her back to the science room. 'So, was his girlfriend with him? The social pages reckon he's split up with that girl from "Home and Away".'

'I'm sure you'll have plenty of time to discuss Dominic Ray's love life at morning tea, Shan.' Mrs Johnson had picked up the conversation as she walked through the door. The class laughed. 'Well done, Nina,' she said as she strode across the classroom. She continued to speak as she dumped her bag on her desk. 'I hope you realise how important your weekend achievements were, young lady. You've taken every girl at Harper one step closer to that elusive introduction to the man himself. They'll all be there to watch you swim next time.' There was a challenge in her words. Looking up and speaking directly to Nina she added, 'I'd make them work for it if I were you.' Nina was positive she saw mischief in her eyes.

Mrs Johnson smiled as she spoke to the class. 'Now, let's try to concentrate, everyone. Page twenty-three of your textbook.'

*

There was always enough time for Nina to get home from school and grab something to eat before heading off to the pool for her afternoon training session. As she walked through the door her elder brother Ryan was making his way from the kitchen to his bedroom eating an overstuffed salad sandwich. Holding it with one hand, his other was held under his chin in an attempt to catch the many stray pieces of lettuce and tomato that fell as he took each bite. 'Messages are all for you,' he said with a full mouth.

Nina made her way around the kitchen grabbing an apple, a plate, a knife, a handful each of a variety of dried fruits and a few crackers before settling down at the breakfast bar with a pen and paper. She cut a slice from her apple and noticed that the machine read eleven. Someone hadn't cleared the messages from yesterday. Nina pressed the button and an un-familiar voice started speaking. Nina gripped the piece of apple with her teeth, dumped the rest of it along with her knife and grabbed the pen.

'I hope I have the right number,' came the voice, efficient yet friendly. 'My name is Jane Prior, producer for "Night Live" on Channel 4. I'm looking for Nina Hallet. If Nina could call me back on 9257 6861 or 0412 975 386 or at home tonight on 9765 2872. Thanks.'

Nina was hurriedly jotting down all the phone numbers when the next message began.

'Andrew Wilcox looking for Nina Hallet.'

And so it went on. Nina's apple was beginning to brown by the time she had listened to the messages. She checked them again to make sure all the numbers were right. She looked at the list. It represented all type of media—TV, radio, news-papers, magazines. They all wanted to interview her. She thought she been pretty well covered over the weekend but she had underestimated the interest in her. 'Backyard and Beyond' had called wanting a story. Like she knew anything about the garden! And 'Cuisine Corner'. Mum would love that. Nina couldn't boil an egg if her life depended on it she would tell people with a laugh. Nina thought she always said it quite proudly. She knew her mum's attitude to cooking. 'The less you knew the better. Then you'll never be a slave in the kitchen,' she'd say, usually as she was pulling something delicious out of the oven. 'Learn to cook for yourself if you must but never let a man know you can cook, take my word.'

'Are you giving her the cooking lecture?' Nina's dad would tease. 'Get barefoot and back into the kitchen before you give our daughter the wrong ideas,' he would joke.

The message that most interested Nina was from *sAssy* magazine. Someone called Tamasin. She hadn't given her last name. But Nina liked the sound of her voice. And *sAssy* was the first magazine purchase Nina had ever made. Might be something interesting she thought.

She looked at her watch. Ten minutes before Jake's mum would be tooting the car horn announcing she and Jake were here to take her to training. It was a car pool arrangement that saw Jake's mum take them to the pool. Nina's dad picked them both up after their workout.

Nina dived into the back of the black Holden a few moments later. She'd quickly changed into her swimsuit, throwing a white turtle neck, grey trackpants and an orange zip-front hooded jacket over the top. Before she had belted up, Jake was telling her about his day.

'You wouldn't believe how many people were asking about you, Nina. People I'd never seen at school before were coming up to me and asking about the weekend and you and talking about how we got in the papers.' There had been a photo of the 'rappers' all hugging Nina after their impromptu performance on the first night had spilled over to the second night when Nina had won the 200m Backstroke as well. The

27

photographers had wanted them to lift Nina in the air for the photo but she had drawn the line at that.

'Same here. All day. I don't see how I'll get any work done this week before I get on that plane to Paris.'

'As if you have to worry about that! Teachers are hardly going to mind.'

'I came home with five million messages that people had left at admin and there were another bunch on the machine when I got there.'

'People?'

'Like journalists or producers.'

'Looks like some of them couldn't wait, Nina.' Mrs Watson, Jake's mother, interrupted their conversation. What was normally a fairly empty parking lot was almost full. Station wagons and odd-looking trucks with satellite dishes on top had taken up just about all of the available spaces. All sorts of camera equipment was on the ground at the feet of the men and women leaning against the cars or talking in groups. They all peered into Mrs Watson's car as it pulled up. As a few of them recognised Nina they began to mobilise. Reporters fixed ties and hair. Camera operators hiked heavy cameras onto their shoulders. Sound operators adjusted headphones.

The three of them sat in the car for a moment. 'Do you want me to come with you, Nina?' Mrs Watson didn't know what she could do except offer her presence as support. Before Nina could answer, Jake did.

'She's an old pro at this, Mum. Aren't you, Nina?'

'Yeah,' she replied, not really listening. She wondered how long it would take to talk to them all. She was supposed to be in the water in five minutes. Better get it over and done with, she thought. She remembered Jake and his mum. 'I'm sure it'll be fine,' she reassured Mrs Watson. 'Maybe you'd could let Mum and Dad know though?' Not that they could do much. But it seemed like the right thing to do.

'I'll call them when I get home, love.'

From the moment Nina opened the door of the car she was being filmed. Jake was at her side in an instant, talking. 'I hate it when they do this. Try to catch me out when I haven't got my look together.' With Nina giggling he continued, 'Oh, did you think they're here to talk to you? Oh gee, Nina, I'm sorry. I should have told you.'

From the opposite direction the reporters began to close in, calling to her.

'Nina, do you mind if we talk to you?'

'Just a few minutes.'

'Nina, before you start training . . .'

'You okay?' Jake in her ear. She nodded. 'Just don't forget to tell them it was my song you were singing when you won your races. They love that stuff.'

She gave him her best 'get-out-of-here' look but he was gone before it landed. She turned her attention back to the advancing throng. Nina wasn't sure where to look or who to speak to so she decided on something general first.

'Hello.' She tried to work out how many of them there were. Maybe twenty-five people. A couple of the faces she recognised from the weekend. There were a few men with cameras standing off to one side, watching. An older man with a moustache was also standing apart from the main group. She smiled at him. She knew he worked for a newspaper although she couldn't remember which one. But he had been very good to talk to over the weekend. He had asked questions that she thought only people who knew about swimming would ask.

With general introductions over, one of the women stepped forward. 'How do you want to do this, Nina? Obviously, we would all like separate interviews. How much time do you have?' The last question was directed at Nina but the woman looked beyond her to the pool entrance.

'Hi, Nina.' Nina had wondered how long it would take him

to find her. She was supposed to be in the water by now. 'Hello, ladies and gentlemen. Jack Saunders. Nina's coach. I know you have a job to do but so do I. And so does Nina. How long are you going to take?'

The woman spoke. 'Jack, Selina Ritchie, "Night Live". We are a national current affairs program, as you no doubt know. We need probably twenty minutes to chat to Nina and then do some filming of her while she trains.' Her voice was smooth as silk now in contrast to the perky way she had addressed Nina.

Jack looked at them all. 'You can film her while she swims as long as that is okay with Nina, but—' he looked at his watch, 'I need her in the water in twenty minutes max so you had all better get your cameras rolling and ask your questions quickly.'

'But . . .' Selina made another attempt but was cut short.

'Will you stay with Nina and be part of the interview, Jack?' Nina knew this man. He was always in the newspapers, not just because he was the star sports reporter on 'A Weekend of Sport', but because he seemed to have a new model on his arm every week.

'It's not me who did the swimming, Tim,' Jack protested.

'But we'd like to ask you a few questions too, Jack.' Tim was using his best coaxing voice now. 'What do you think, Nina?'

Nina jumped at the sound of her name. She had been watching the proceedings as though she was a mere spectator. 'What do you say to letting us give the old guy the third degree?' Tim Benson was using his coaxing voice on her now.

'As long as I don't pay for it later!' she shot back without thinking. It got a laugh.

'All right, let's get going.' Tim Benson had taken over. Nina looked at Selina. She wasn't happy. Nina made a mental note to answer her questions as well as she possibly could.

'Nina, the day after your great performances on the weekend, how are you feeling?' Tim Benson got the first question in.

'It doesn't feel like it's happening to me yet. It's like I'm watching someone else. But I guess Jack will make sure I know it's happening to me when I go back into hard training tonight to get ready for Manchester.' She shot Jack a look and everyone laughed.

'How did everyone react at school?'

'They were pretty into it. Suddenly everyone knew me, which was funny. But, umm, usual stuff, I guess. Special assembly. All that.' Nina thought of Mrs Johnson. 'Basically the girls wanted to know about Dominic Ray and the boys about Inga Holder.' Another laugh. She was starting to get the hang of this.

'Does the inclusion of Inga Holder make you feel under-rated? The selectors are basically saying you are a fluke, aren't they?' The question was from Selina Ritchie.

Before Nina had a chance to respond Jack had exploded. 'What sort of a question is that to ask Nina? Nina beat her fair and square and she'll do it again.'

'I'm not saying she didn't,' Selina came back at him. 'I'm just saying the selectors don't seem to think so, Jack. Maybe you are a little too close to Nina to be objective.'

'What are you suggesting now?' Jack shot back. The coach and reporter glared at one another.

Nina jumped in with the best thing she could think of. 'You know, I think we were talking about this in social science today. Sort of. In regard to things like long term unemployment and whether experience is valued. And how even in the media it's all about the "new young thing". I think that is what you are asking me, Selina. Do I think experience is valuable? I think, yes, definitely. Inga is a great champion. And Jebby. And I hope to learn things from them. You know, if they want to teach a kid. I'm glad she has been selected.'

Selina just looked at Nina and nodded. Jack looked at her in astonishment, wondering where the little girl he had coached for two years had gone. Nina had no idea that in one moment she had changed everyone's opinion of her. She remembered the other part of the question.

'As far as the fluke thing goes, umm, well I hope I'm not a fluke.' She laughed but no one laughed with her. She looked at Jack. 'I'll just keep doing what I've been doing until now. Train hard and go as fast as I can in my races. That's all I can do, isn't it?' Jack nodded and smiled in agreement. Nina thought he looked really uncomfortable. She felt sorry for him.

'Did you check out the virtual tour of Manchester, Nina?' Nina recognised the newspaperman's voice.

'I did. Thank you for that.' She explained to the others. 'This man, umm . . . Mr . . .?'

'Ron Samuels. Call me Ron, Nina.'

'Oh, okay. Umm, well, Ron told me about the virtual tour of the Commonwealth Games site on the Net. Have any of you looked at it?' There were a few shaking heads. 'Oh, well you've got to! It's wicked! Dad and I looked at it. The English swimmers all say the pool is fast as! And the stadium is even bigger than ours. The thought of walking in there for the opening ceremony is a bit of a head spin.' She laughed at the thought. 'I didn't look for a virtual tour of the Athletic Institute in Paris where we are in camp. But I've got enough to check out in Paris, if we have time. Mum works in a dress shop in Harper Bay and makes our clothes and stuff so she knows all about Paris. I have to take lots of notes on how all the Parisian girls dress. And Jake,' she looked back toward the pool where she had left him, 'you know he is our resident homey. He's into hip-hop and stuff and I think that Manchester is a pretty good place for all of that. And Dad's a Man U fan so I'll have to get him an authentic jersey from there. So . . . it's going to be great.'

Now it did seem as though all this was happening to her.

'Although I'll miss Mum and Dad. But then, I am getting eight weeks off school!' She laughed again. It was more like an impish chuckle that brought her shoulders to her ears and squashed her dark curls in the process. Just as quickly a serious thought flashed across her face. 'But don't tell Mum I said that!' She saw Ron Samuels grin as he made notes.

Selina smiled. Tim looked at Nina as though he hadn't understood a word she had said. She looked at Jack. He was shuffling his feet and looking serious again. She hoped she hadn't said the wrong thing.

'I should probably get into training, huh?' she asked him. He nodded.

'Is that okay?' But she wasn't really asking them. She was ready to get into the pool. The comfort of doing something more familiar was suddenly very appealing.

'That's plenty, Nina.' Selina wasn't putting on any voice now. When she added, 'You were really terrific. Thanks,' she sounded genuine.

CHAPTER THREE

BONJOUR sAssy *READERS!*

I've never kept a diary before but since you guys seem to be so interested in what I'm up to I'll give it a go.

We are in Paris for a three week training camp before the Commonwealth Games in Manchester.

As you can imagine, Paris has been really tough to take! Every known variety of pastry for breakfast, a breathtaking city to see and a bit of swimming now and then! Yesterday was a rest day. I went with a couple of the girls to look at all the beautiful salons of the famous fashion houses. When we got to Jean-Paul Gaultier's salon (we don't use the word shop here in Paris!) there was a surprise for us. Inga Holder's manager had called and let them know that some of the Australian swimming team were going to visit and as a result Monsieur Gaultier himself was there to meet us. Although he insisted we call him Jean-Paul! He was so nice.

As you can see from the photos I took with the sAssy camera, he let us try on heaps of his beautiful clothes. Because Inga is like a model anyway he had her try on one of the dresses they were making for this season's couture (glad I can write the word rather than say it!) collections. Apparently it was worth about $20 000 dollars. Isn't it breathtaking? Thanks to Inga, sAssy readers are the first to see it.

Then to me, Jean-Paul said, 'You'll grow into this stuff in a few years curly-top . . . for now we have some fun!' And he took me to another room that was full of the funkiest clothes—wild colours and crazy stripes. As you can see, he took a photo every time I changed outfits. He gave us an outfit each. A good luck token. The photo of all of us together shows us in our new clothes. Inga, Stella Owens and Jessica Hall are the other 'models'. You can imagine how jealous the rest of the team was when we got back to the hotel.

Au revoir *for now!*

AUSTRALIA ON TARGET FOR RECORD GOLD MEDAL HAUL
by Ron Samuels

Paris. Sunday. The Australian swimming team wrapped up its two week training camp in Paris today with a sizzling session of time trials that left swimmers and coaches alike wearing broad grins.

'I've never seen a team like it,' said Head Coach Brian Cook. 'Obviously I've travelled with many of the swimmers before to other events. But the newcomers who have been added to the team for the Commonwealth Games give it a strength and depth that is really exciting to watch.'

One of the newcomers is the little fourteen-year-old backstroker, Nina Hallet.

'She bounces around the pool like a jack-in-the-box,' said Cook, 'she's that excited. I think her enthusiasm has had an effect on everybody, even the most jaded.'

But it's Hallet's efforts in the pool that have everyone talking. Brian Cook has no doubt of what she is capable. 'We have to be careful not to put too much pressure on her. This is her first international competition and it's a big one. But if she can handle it mentally, then no one will get near her.'

Greetings sAssy *readers*

Finally we reach Manchester for the Commonwealth Games. I was a bit sorry to leave Paris, although I'm sure the Parisians weren't sorry to see the back of me. I carried my French phrase book around religiously and tried hard to master the language. The Parisians usually let me have a go, corrected my pronunciation, then had a laugh at my expense and answered in English anyway!

At least in Manchester language won't be a barrier. Having said that, the accent is kind of weird!

The athletes village is massive. Thousands of athletes from all over the Commonwealth—it's almost too much to comprehend!

Yesterday I was standing in line at the cafeteria and there was a mountain of a man in front of me. I wondered what sport he could possibly do until someone yelled out, 'Hey, Declan, bring more bread!'

I realised that I was standing behind Declan Sinclair, the Olympic champion decathlete. Was I allowed to get his auto-graph or was that not the cool thing to do? Should he be free of autograph hunters inside the village at least? You can imagine my dilemma, dear sAssy readers!

I was still pondering this when I heard a deep voice beside me say, 'If it's not one thing it's another.' I looked up and he was smiling at me. I couldn't think of anything funny to say so I just said, 'Yeah, useless, huh!' But he laughed and then we had a bit more of a chat. I told him it was my first Games and he told me to keep a diary so I remember everything because there was lots that he forgot about the first time. I told him I was doing that. He wished me luck and left with the hugest amount of food on his tray—and lots of bread!

I have spoken to my first Olympic champion! I'm sure I won't be able to sleep tonight!

Dear sAssy readers

A short entry because I don't have a lot of time today. I am trying to have a sleep before the final of the 100m Backstroke tonight. I'm swimming the final from lane four. That means I swam the fastest in the heats this morning. I don't know whether I am totally numb or totally calm. I am having trouble sleeping which means I must be a little bit nervous. But apart from that, it all feels perfectly natural. Weird! Will let you know how I go.

P.S. I've included a few photos of the team in different stages *of preparation: trying on our Commonwealth Games team uniform (where was Jean-Paul when we needed him!); on the field of the stadium after we marched in the opening ceremony (awesome), and team members watching from the pool deck as others begin their Commonwealth Games campaigns. Their faces say it all, don't they?*

SCHOOLGIRL SENSATION A GAMES HIT!

by Ron Samuels

Manchester. Tuesday. In the first real upset at the Manchester Commonwealth Games, pretty Sydney schoolgirl Nina Hallet stormed home to win a gold medal for Australia in the Women's 100m Backstroke today.

Competing at her first international swimming meet, Hallet swam the race like a seasoned professional. Letting the rest of the field lead her through the first half of the race she seemed to move into top gear after the 50m turn. As the others faded Hallet employed a powerful kick in the final stages that left the other swimmers in her wake. Although team coaches were predicting a strong performance from Hallet, no one expected she would defeat a field of considerable experience, including Australian Olympian, Inga Holder. Holder finished third behind English swimmer Sharon Caulfield.

For a few moments after the race, Hallet seemed genuinely stunned. 'Everything is happening so fast,' she admitted to journalists at the post-race press conference, all of them eager to find out something about the little girl with the Luna Park grin. 'I mean, I wish I could tell you why this is happening. In the last couple of weeks everything has just clicked and I feel like I hardly touch the water when I'm in it. I guess it's just a lot of hard work in training finally paying off. Whatever it is, it's just the best!' she added with a giggle that had the usually solemn press corp joining in.

LISA FORREST

NINA DOES IT AGAIN!
by Ron Samuels

Manchester. Thursday. Proving her win in the 100m was anything but a fluke, Commonwealth Champion Nina Hallet added another gold medal to her tally when she won the 200m Backstroke here at the Manchester Aquatic Centre tonight. The dark-haired dynamo had the whole crowd jumping up and cheering her on as she swam a time just four-tenths of a second outside the world record to win another gold medal for Australia.

'I always feel more confident about the 200m. I'm just better at it. Everyone was saying, "oh you let the others go out hard in the 100m" but I knew that I was just trying to wind up and get going! I'm not really a sprinter. I've got a bit more time in the 200m. I like that.'

Hallet seems to finally be getting used to the idea of winning. On Tuesday night she appeared to be looking around for confirmation that she had won her first race. Tonight she confidently glided back down the pool to where the Australian team was sitting, and gave them a wave.

'Well, you don't get lessons in how to behave when you win a race at the Commonwealth Games, do you,' she giggled when asked about her new found comfort with winning. 'And sometimes you watch people and it seems like a bit of a carry on, doesn't it? But Dominic and some of the other swimmers suggested that I at least enjoy it for a few moments. So I tried to do that tonight. I tried to imagine Mum and Dad watching on the telly. I waved so that they could see me.'

Hello again sAssy *readers!*

First I have to say thank you so much for all of the e-mails, herogrammes and letters you have sent to me in the last weeks. I get pathetically homesick and it always makes me feel better to hear from someone at home.

As you probably know by now, I have won a couple of races at the Commonwealth Games and suddenly I am being treated like a movie star. We have had invitations to all sorts of parties and clubs and stuff in Manchester. I haven't been able to go to many of them though. I've been selected in the Australian team

38

MAKING THE MOST OF IT

for the World Championships, which follow the Commonwealth
Games in two weeks time in Los Angeles. So I have to get back
into training straight away. But we have done some fun things
in Manchester. The final night of the swimming we went to a
club called Deca-Dance and danced all night to some really
wicked music. I am not as good at naming music as my friend at
swimming training, Jake, but I would say it was a little bit of
house, a little bit of jungle and some generally phat sounds. I
hope that makes sense!

We did a bit of shopping in Manchester. I bought the coolest
dress. Had to check with Mum that I could spend all of my
savings on it. Really girlie, halter-neck frill and swirling florals
that look great with my European summer tan!

And we got to meet some of the Manchester United FA cup
team and I got some autographs for Dad.

Speaking of autographs, you'll never guess what happened! I
was signing some myself when I got back to the village after I
won the 200m (so you see it is okay to ask for an autograph in
the village), when I heard this, 'Hey, I know you!'

It was Declan Sinclair! He said, 'You didn't tell me you were
going to blast everyone out of the water, Miss Nina Hallet. I
want your autograph!' He has the best laughing eyes. So I
gathered up all my courage and said, 'Only if I can have your
autograph, Mr Declan Sinclair.' He said, 'Deal!' We traded
baseball caps as well. When he left he said, 'See you at the
Olympics, Nina Hallet!' The Olympics, can you imagine?

Hey there, all my sAssy friends!

Hiya from Hollywood. That seems to be the way you are
greeted here. 'Hiyahowyadoin?' All one word. As you have
guessed, we are now here in LA or 'La La Land' as some of the
team like to joke.

Very different to Paris and London, but still interesting.
Talking purely food, we have been on a slow decline since

39

leaving Paris. Probably a good thing though. Without a heavy training schedule, too much good food can be an unnecessary temptation.

Many of the Australian team have been to LA before and they have promised that we will do a theme park tour before we leave. A few great rollercoaster rides would make the trip just perfect!

I don't know what to expect from my swimming. I have never had to back up again and again for major meets and try to swim best times. An occasional National Championship doesn't really prepare you for Commonwealth Games one week and World Championships the next!

A girl called Rain Summers is the world record holder in both of the backstroke races and there is a girl from the Czech Republic that is, apparently, really good too.

One of the nice things is the way that each championship has been like a reunion for many of the swimmers. Even though they race against each other, they seem to be genuinely happy to see one another and catch up with everything that has been happening. When the Games were over in Manchester, everyone was talking about seeing one another in two weeks in LA and how good it would be. So even though you read about rivalry in the newspapers it is really only a small part of it. I have met so many people. I just hope I can remember everyone's names when I see them again this week at the pool in LA!

Got to go and workout!

WORLD JUST OUT OF NINA'S REACH!

by Ron Samuels

Los Angeles. Sunday. Australia's newest swimming sensation, Nina Hallet, had her barnstorming gold medal campaign halted today—but only just. Coming home hard in what is becoming her trademark style, the Harper High beauty with the Clara Bow curls lunged at the finish line to come second to American Rain

Summers in the 100m Backstroke at the World Championships. But with only two-tenths of a second separating Hallet and the reigning Olympic champion, the young Australian served notice that she will be the one to beat come the Olympic Games in two years' time.

The Australian head coach Brian Cook was ecstatic about his young charge's performance. 'I kept telling myself she is only young, you can't expect too much. But she has a focus way beyond her years. She has come away from this trip with the whole world wanting to know more about her.'

Nina herself wasn't so sure. 'I guess I got a bit too used to winning at the Commonwealth Games. I kept saying I didn't know what to expect of myself but having gone so close to the gold medal I am a bit disappointed that I couldn't find that little extra bit from somewhere. But then, I did my best time again so I can't be too disappointed, can I?'

WORLD RECORD NOT GOOD ENOUGH FOR NINA
by Ron Samuels

Los Angeles. Wednesday. Australia's Nina Hallet learned one of the harsh realities of sport here at the World Swimming Championships today: sometimes breaking a world record isn't enough. In a thrilling 200m Backstroke Final Hallet swam stroke for stroke with the Olympic champion Rain Summers, fading in the last ten metres to finish second to the American. But only after both girls had broken the existing world record. Summers added her own voice to the chorus that has followed Hallet when she declared after the race, 'I'd never heard of her. Where did she come from?'

Hallet, who had been a little despondent after her silver medal in the 100m Backstroke, was back to her best tonight. Leaning down to receive her medal on the dais, the Sydney teenager seemed to have an unusually animated chat to Gianfranco Rinaldi, the FINA swimming president making the presentation. In a move that delighted the crowd at the Los Angeles International Aquatic Centre, she then pulled a pocket-sized camera from her jacket—an item you rarely see her without—and handed it to the president who took a snap of the three medal winners. Asked at the post-race press conference if her world record-breaking swim was the highlight of her first international swimming tour she replied, with all sincerity, 'Oh no. Last night we met Julia Roberts.' The grin that followed would have given the famous actress a run for her money.

Hi sAssy *readers*

My final entry because we are heading home tonight.

I can't wait to get home and see Mum and Dad and tell them about everything that has happened. Even though I have e-mailed regularly, there are still lots more stories.

We finally got to do the tour of the theme parks. We had a couple of free days after the World Championships so everyone was free to do their own thing. A couple of the older swimmers were as keen as I was to do a rollercoaster comparison, so we went to Magic Mountain and Disneyland. I don't think I can choose. They were all awesome. But I think my stomach will be happy to have a rest from crazy rides for a while.

I have included a variety of photos from Los Angeles, not just at the pool but also of our time off. My favourite is of the photographers taking photos of Rain Summers, Ursula Rekic and me after the 200m Backstroke. I didn't know whether I was allowed to take my camera with me for my races but I took a chance on the last race because, well, it was my last chance. No one seemed to mind. I also like the photo of our 'veteran' dis-tance swimmer, Jill Banks. A veteran at 25! I think the look on her face says everything. She has just won the 400m Freestyle. Having announced her retirement after this meet she looks happy she has won, sad it's for the last time and relieved that she has finished a winner.

Our plane is boarding. I've got to go!

CHAPTER FOUR

THE LIGHTS IN the room gradually dimmed. There was a corresponding increase in the noise in the room, but Nina and her mother knew this was only momentary. They had watched the ritual a few times now. Sitting in the VIP section meant their seats were secure but it made observation a little difficult. Nina figured it was one of the trade-offs. It lessened her chances of a good photo. Not that she was taking photos for *sAssy* anymore but she had found the habit difficult to give up, even if she had wanted to.

'Nina,' came a voice from behind her. She knew that voice. Up until a week ago she could have walked out of her hotel room and into his down the corridor to have breakfast.

'Hi, Dominic.'

'See how fickle fame is,' he joked. 'Last year I had front row seats and now I have to sit behind some fourteen-year-old superstar!'

'They didn't want to waste their seats this year on Neanderthals who will never work out how to dress,' she smiled sweetly.

Dominic smiled sweetly back. He was sitting with a beautiful blonde girl who looked like a model. There wasn't a chance for introductions. At that moment the room reverberated with the opening beat of a song and hundreds of searchlights criss-crossed the room. And then it was under way. Models sashaying down the catwalk, flashbulbs going off, people clapping.

43

Nina looked at her mum. Her eyes were darting every-where, trying to take it all in. This was the fifth show they had been to in Fashion Week and her mother was still as awed as she had been at the first. Not that Nina wasn't, but she liked to watch her mother enjoy it all. She was glad she had brought her. She was always going to, from the moment the invitation from the designer arrived, along with an outfit to wear to the show. But she was even more sure it was the right choice when a weekly magazine had written a story about her and Jake. All because he had accompanied her to a few of the events she had been invited to when she got back from her trip.

One was to the premiere of an action film made in Sydney. At the party after the film she and Jake had made a pact to try every canapé that went by on a tray, even if they didn't like the look of it. The faces each had pulled on tasting some of the morsels had been more entertaining than the film.

Two nights later they went to the Australian Music Industry Awards. Nina thought Jake might meet some people who could help him. She had laughed when a woman from the magazine had approached her at the Awards and asked if Jake was her boyfriend. It was too ridiculous to contemplate. But she should have denied it more strenuously. When the story came out they had called him Nina's constant companion. Jake, of all people!

She had told Jake about the woman and her question on the way home from the Awards. She assumed he would laugh too. But he got upset.

'Why is it so ridiculous, Nina?'

'Because.' She couldn't think of anything else to say. His reaction made her uncomfortable. And he should know why. Jake was her friend. He wasn't her boyfriend. He was funny and goofy, not the sort of person she was attracted to. In the boyfriend way. But she couldn't say any of that to him. ''Cause. We're friends, that's all. Aren't we?'

'Yeah, we're friends.' He had looked out of the window of

the limousine that was taking them home. 'But you didn't have to tell her that it was ridiculous,' he added quietly.

He hadn't called her since then and they usually talked everyday. She thought it would be better if she waited a while before asking him to anything else. It was a waste though. Both of them were on their three-week break from swimming, a rest they took at the end of every season. And there were so many invitations.

She couldn't take her brother. She was never sure whether he would talk to her from one day to the next. Which was the way it always was but it seemed worse since she'd got back from the trip.

And she had to be careful with the girls from school because it seemed if you asked one then you were obliged to make it up to someone else the next time. Unless she asked Alice. But Alice wasn't really the person you would want at every event. Like the ticker-tape parade the team had been given when they got back home.

Harper High had organised buses for the students who wanted to go to the city for the parade. Many of the students had made the trip, including Shan, Ruby and their followers. And, of course, Alice. Even with the noise of thousands of people who lined George Street, it was Alice's cries that brought the Harper High contingent to Nina's attention as they travelled along the parade route in open top cars.

'Neeeeeeennaaaaaah!'

Nina had turned to see Alice's red face leaning way over the barricade in an effort to make Nina see her.

'I think that girl knows you,' Dominic had said to Nina as he nudged her. She was sandwiched between Dominic Ray and Mark Highbury, the Commonwealth and World 200m Freestyle champion for Australia. Any girl would be happy with the seating arrangement and Nina was doubly so when she saw Shan and Ruby standing behind Alice.

After the parade she had introduced as many of the Harper students as she could to the swimmers. Until she herself had been mobbed by the crowds. No matter how many people crowded around her she could hear Alice's screech every time she met another member of the team. Sometimes Alice's enthusiasm was a little bit too much. Even for Nina.

A nudge from Nina's mother brought her back to the show. One of the models on stage was wearing the exact outfit Nina had on. As she strode down the runway her eyes met Nina's and she gave her a wink. Nina was mesmerised. The girl couldn't have been much older than Nina but she had a haughtiness in her walk that made Nina sit up straighter in her chair without even being conscious of it. It wasn't until her mother gave her another nudge that Nina realised she was trying to emulate the girl's posture.

'You look like C3PO,' her mother whispered.

Nina shrunk down in her seat hoping all eyes were on the girl on the catwalk rather than her own poor imitation.

After the show, they bumped into Dominic again and Nina introduced him to her mother.

'Have you been to see Sam yet?' he asked Nina.

'Tomorrow, after school.' To her mother, she said, 'I told you Sam Thompson is Dominic's manager, didn't I?'

Her mother nodded.

'I'm sure you'll feel more comfortable with him, Mrs Hallet,' Dominic assured her. Nina had told him about some of their experiences so far. 'As I explained to Nina, as a swimmer he has been through it all himself. He just knows what he's talking about. But don't take my word for it.'

Nina watched her mother absorb Dominic's words. 'Anything would be an improvement on the used car dealers who have approached us so far, Dominic. We just don't have the luxury of time. Every day someone else calls wanting Nina to do something for them. They all want decisions and they don't want to hear we're talking to potential managers.'

'They want Nina, Mrs Hallet. They have to wait. But Sam will sort all that out for you.'

*

Sam Thompson opened the glass door to his office as Nina and her parents emerged from the lift.

'Hi,' he called to them. 'I'm Sam.' He shook their hands as they filed through the door. 'Come in. It doesn't look too inspiring, I know. We have just moved in, so please excuse the mess,' he explained as Nina and her parents looked for a place to stand amidst boxes, filing cabinets and desks. A couple of people worked at putting the office into shape and giving it some life. Nina smiled at them before turning back to look at Sam Thompson. He had the tall, broad-shouldered, gangly look of a swimmer. Dominic had told her that Sam had been a backstroker too, 'when you were still in nappies'. She knew this was an exaggeration. He looked fit enough to get in the water and swim for Australia that day. He looked at them with an open face and grin that suited his sandy, almost surfer-like features.

'Um, well, I'm Nina and this is my mum and dad.'

'Geoff is my name, Sam,' her dad said and put his hand out to shake Sam's, forgetting they had already done it. When he realised what he was doing, he laughed as they all did and placed his hand back by his side. 'Sorry, um, and this is my wife, Annette,' he said with a little less confidence.

Nina smiled encouragingly at her Dad, knowing that meeting new people made him more nervous than just about anything else.

'Well, let's go into my office for a chat,' Sam said, leading the way. 'The last couple of months must have made you pretty proud of your daughter,' he went on as they moved into a smaller room with floor to ceiling windows that looked west over the harbour and beyond. He motioned them to sit in the comfortable lounge chairs around a large coffee table that displayed afternoon tea for four.

'We're always pretty proud of her, Sam,' her dad answered. Nina's mother nodded.

'Understandably,' he nodded, smiling at Nina. 'Swimming in the family?

'Not me,' Nina's mother joined the conversation. 'Nina gets it from Geoff.'

'Hardly. I've been in the surf club since I was a kid, but I wasn't much of swimmer,' he explained to Sam. 'Nina and I used to go down and swim 400m at the local rock pool, you know, after school. She was beating me by the time she was about eight. The blokes at the club used to give me a bit of a hard time. But I thought she was great.'

Typical, Nina thought, we all worry Dad will be too nervous to speak and then we can't keep him quiet.

'What about you, Nina,' Sam brought her into the conversation. 'What do you like to do beside swim?'

It wasn't the question she was expecting. 'Oh, lots of things. I read, and Mum and I sew a bit. Clothes and stuff. Travel, now after my trip. I could really get into that. And art. I like art history at school. But I'm not very good at the practical side. Unless you count taking photos. I like that. I had to do a bit of that while I was away but I don't know if you call it art.'

'Sure you do,' Sam countered. 'What do you like? Landscape? Portraits?'

'Oh, portraits, well people, I guess. I haven't got to landscapes.'

'Well,' he craned his neck up to look through the windows out to the offices. 'Once we get ourselves set up out there you'll see a few Ansell Adams. He was into landscapes. National parks, Yosemite. Black and whites. Beautiful. But I've also got a book on Man Ray. You can have a look at it if

48

you want. But there are lots of great photographers. The wonderful thing about your swimming is it'll take you to cities all over the world.' He leaned back in his chair and motioned out through the windows of the office. 'Cities that hold the greatest collections of everything you could ever want to know about. Everywhere you go there will be something new and inspiring.'

He looked back around the room and smiled at Nina. No one said anything for a moment. Then her mother spoke.

'Are you interested in photography too, Sam?'

'Sure. Lots of things. If there was one thing my mother was adamant about it was that swimming was only part of my life. It's not your future, she would say. Indirectly it is now, with what I do. But it didn't have to be. I didn't forsake everything for it. And that was really important to her.'

Nina relaxed into the soft chair. How well she knew that argument. She didn't have to look at her mother and father to know that Sam Thompson had just become her new manager.

CHAPTER FIVE

NINA YAWNED AND rubbed her eyes.

'Back in training, Nina?' Although the voice was gentle, it made Nina jump. She thought she was alone in the classroom. She opened her eyes to find Mrs Johnson sitting on the edge of the desk in front of Nina's.

Nina nodded in response. 'Sorry, I was just finishing that last problem.' She jumped up and began packing up her books. 'I didn't think anyone was still around.' She was telling the truth. Although she was in no hurry to leave the classroom. The energy required for lunchtime conversation felt beyond her today.

'I've got to lock the science rooms at lunch so I can't go until you do.' Mrs Johnson watched Nina put the books in her bag. 'You okay? You look tired.'

'Yeah. Good. Just training, as you said.' Nina didn't look at Mrs Johnson as she spoke. She didn't want to bring any undue attention to herself. She certainly didn't want any reports getting back to her mother that her new life was detrimental to her schoolwork. 'It's always a bit hard to get back into it when you've had a break,' she added. She gave Mrs Johnson a smile for added reassurance. Keeping aside the paper bag that contained her lunch, she finished buckling her bag and made her way past her science teacher.

'And I imagine going back to the old routine must be a bit tough after all the excitement you've seen in the last couple of months.'

Nina's first thought was that her mother had already spoken to Mrs Johnson. In a split second she was back in the kitchen of her home the previous afternoon. Her body had suddenly started to shake and tears flooded from her eyes as though the levies that had held them in place had been bulldozed in one giant push. Thing was, she hadn't even known there were any levies. Hadn't known there was a torrent of water to hold back. And for no apparent reason. She had gone to the cupboard and found the tupperware container empty of sultanas, her usual afternoon snack before training. But it wasn't a legitimate reason to start crying. Her mum didn't ask any questions. Just slowly moved toward her and put her arm around her shoulders. That had produced another gush of water.

'I don't know why this is happening.' Nina had tried to laugh through the tears but it wasn't convincing the bulldozers.

'It's just a kind of let down, I guess, Neen.' Her mother rarely dropped the second syllable of Nina's name. And didn't let anyone else do it if she could help it. 'Hmm?' She ran her hands through Nina's hair. 'You had to come back to earth at some point, sweetie. And you went up so high. The landing was going to be hard.'

Nina was confused. Her mind had kept her feelings a secret from her body. Or was it the other way around? And how had her mother known? And now her teacher?

'It is a bit weird,' she admitted to Mrs Johnson who was still leaning on the desk watching her.

Mrs Johnson just nodded and smiled.

Nina left the classroom and walked slowly along the empty corridor, enjoying the weight of the dark cold cement that surrounded her. The strange thing was that even though she had been shaken by the outburst, she felt better afterwards.

Later, in training, her body was more responsive than it had been for ages. Since before the trip, maybe. It felt free to be strained with the force of exercise. And how good it felt to once again put her body under that strain. She was in the endurance phase of her workout cycle. Four weeks of long, hard kilometres. She pushed her body until it burned. Exhaustion meant she was left retching over the toilet bowl after the session but she felt better.

'That's a bit more like it, Nina,' Jack had said as she passed him on the way out. She nodded in agreement. She was back in control.

Even she and Jake had talked last night. Polite would have been the best way to describe their exchanges as they first began to travel to training again. But last night they had continued a conversation during the entire session. Quick comments snatched, often out of breath, in between laps. At one point, Jack even suggested they stop talking and concentrate on what they were doing. The shared moment of indignation seemed to edge them closer together. I hope so, Nina thought as she made her way to the Year 9 lunch area.

'She's definitely changed though.' Nina heard Ruby Wilcox's voice before she rounded the corner. Something about it made her stop before she was seen.

'Like, what about the ticker-tape thing. 'Member, Shan? You even said she was sitting in between those guys like she was, I dunno, Claire Danes or someone.'

Nina fell back against the wall as if she'd been hit.

'It's that don't-I-have-the-cutest-smile thing that makes me want to throw up.' The lazy tones of Shan's voice made it sound as though it was a subject she was over-discussing.

'Ha! Well, you guys have bought into the whole thing.' The challenge came from Sharon Little. During the small amount of time Nina had spent within the hang, Sharon was the only girl she'd heard disagree with Shan and Ruby. 'If I remember correctly, you couldn't wait to get to the parade. You didn't

52

find me down on my knees going, "oohh Nina, oohh Dominic, my new best friends", Like I said, anyone who has to resort to sport is too dumb to do anything else.'

There was silence for a moment. Nina could imagine Shan standing, one arm across her chest twirling her cigarette lighter, the other resting on the crossed arm as she dragged deeply from the lit cigarette, giving her time to think of an answer.

'I only went so I could have the day off,' was the best Shan could offer.

'Yeah right,' Nina said to herself. She imagined rounding the corner and saying it to all of them, 'That's why you nearly wet yourself when you met Dominic.' She could see herself tossing her head back and standing there defiantly so they'd all know that she'd heard them. She wanted to do it but her mind could not will her body into action. She slammed her fist against the wall, remembering too late she was holding the bag that contained her lunch.

'Idiot,' she berated herself. She pushed off the wall. But rather than acting out her thoughts she headed in the opposite direction, back toward the quadrangle. She shook her head as she walked. She remembered how thrilled she'd been when Shan had asked her to come and hang with them.

'Idiot,' she said it a bit louder this time, not caring who heard her. She was moving with no destination in mind. But her body instinctively took her along corridors that wound away from the areas students congregated for lunch.

'It's your own fault,' the dialogue continued, 'they talk about others, they were bound to talk about you.' Now her voice had become her mother's. Her bag fell from her shoulder. She threw it against the wall in disgust. She looked around to find herself upstairs in the language block. Good, she was sure to be left alone.

Her mother hadn't been impressed when Nina told her she

had been invited to sit with Shan and the others. She had been less impressed when Nina casually repeated the gossip that had been discussed at lunch one day.

'Do you know that for a fact?' her mother asked when Nina had told her a story about Nell Hopper's brother who had been caught shoplifting. 'And even if it is true, are you going to judge Nell for something her brother did? Doesn't sound like you, Nina.'

She listened more carefully to the lunchtime talk after that. Rarely were the comments complimentary. When she told her mother this, she merely raised her eyebrows and said, 'This surprises you, sweetheart?'

But it did surprise Nina. These girls had everything. They were good-looking. They had great clothes to wear. Their families seemed to have enough money. More than her family, she was sure of that. And they could always think of the right thing to say, especially to boys. But when she argued those points with her mother the only response she got was, 'ah-huh.'

Nina sat on her bag and leaned against the wall. Her mind went back to the conversation she had just heard. She thought of the ticker-tape parade. Had she behaved like some sort of poser? Like she thought she was something special? Maybe she had. She remembered having a great time. And she did feel special sitting up in the cars with all of those people cheering. Maybe she had waved too much or something. Had she become a show-off? But surely her mum and dad would have said something. She had been doing a lot of unusual things since she'd been back. Meeting a lot of famous people and stuff. Maybe she did talk about it too much. But the girls were always asking questions. Maybe it would be better not to say anything. She didn't know what to do. She wanted her brain to stop thinking. She was getting a headache. She rested her head in her hands and massaged her temples with her fingertips.

As her thoughts slowed down she became aware of music coming from somewhere. Someone was practising the piano. Occasionally the sound would stop. A couple of notes would be played again, then again. And then the music would continue. Nina didn't like the music much but she admired the playing. It sounded quite difficult. Something classical she guessed, although she knew nothing about classical music. 'Too dumb to do anything else.' Sharon Little's words came back to Nina.

'Stupid *and* a show-off,' she said to herself and anyone else who was listening, 'can't get much worse than that, ninja-girl.' The voice in her head was so good at summing things up. Her breath shortened, sharpened, caught in the back of her throat.

'Idiot,' she said again, attempting to regain control. She tried to force herself to breathe deeply. The music didn't help. The repetition, the short notes. But at least it demanded her attention. Gradually the playing became more fluid. The sound reverberated from the instrument through the concrete halls and through her body. She got up, grabbed her bag and moved toward the sound.

On the other side of the walkway she paused outside the music room. She could see him bent over the keys. It was his hands that she noticed first. His energy was like a funnel, filtering down through his body until it was suitably refined to flow out through his long, elegant fingers. Every muscle in the hand was poised, controlled, on notice to glide over the keys and stroke which ever one was necessary to bring forth the required sound.

The pianist faltered over another note and the music stopped. Nina's fixation with his hands was broken. Catching herself staring, her eyes flew to his face. At the same moment, the pianist looked up. Nina realised it was the new boy. What was his name? He had been in a couple of her classes. He looked at her with a gaze that suggested she was intruding.

'Ah, that was, um, you know, very nice,' was all she could stammer. She regretted it the moment the words left her lips.

His body shifted slightly. If his look was now meant to indicate she was pathetic, it worked.

'Only someone who knew nothing about music would call Beethoven "nice".' He turned away from her and began to riffle through a pile of music books stacked on the piano.

Nina felt a wave of heat move from her toes all the way up her body. Her skin prickled. Her heart raced. Whether it was delayed reaction to the conversation she had overheard not so long ago, or the flick of his head when he said the word 'nice', she wasn't sure. She just knew she had to say something. Anything.

'Well, only someone who knew nothing about anything would be rude when they were being paid a compliment!' She said it quietly. Not for effect, but to hide her cracking voice.

He turned back to look at her. He said nothing. But he was without the attitude he had just displayed. She held her ground for a moment before walking off.

'About time,' she said to herself. After a few casual steps she broke into a run. She needed to find a bathroom and wash her face before her tears gave her away.

CHAPTER SIX

THE BRICK WALL was just a little too high to be really comfortable. But it was wide enough to rest her lunch on. And it
was in the shade. The wind brought a waft of something quite
sweet. Maybe the wattle, Nina thought, noticing the flowering
tree close to the wall.

She was pretty pleased with her new lunchtime spot, her
own private hang. Sitting alone wasn't perfect, but it was
better than being fake friends with Shan and the others. And
it wasn't like before the Commonwealth Games. Then, not
having anyone to sit with at lunch made Nina feel like a real
loser. Now, no one thought of her as that. And apart from
these lunches she was definitely not alone.

In fact, life had become so busy in the months since the
Games and World Championships that the forty minute
lunch break was often the only time she had to herself. And
the months ahead were going to be even busier. Once there
had been a few local swimming races, State Championships
and maybe the National Championships to look forward to
over the summer. Now there were training camps with the
national swim team—of which Nina was a member—and
swim meets all over the world she was expected to compete
in. She was always being invited to parties and premieres and
other events. There were lunch and dinner engagements she
was asked to speak at, sponsors' events to attend, interviews
with the media, school work to complete. And letters—more
letters than she could ever hope to answer.

She squirmed to the back of the ledge, brought her legs up and crossed them under her. She dragged a purple manila folder out of her bag. Sam had finally convinced Nina that a form letter was the only way to keep on top of her fan mail. She hadn't finished signing the letters last night before bed, so she had brought the rest to school to do during lunch. It wasn't something she would want anyone to see her doing.

Suddenly a branch broke behind her. Her body jumped with surprise and the manila folder slid off her lap. In slow motion she watched the loose sheets of paper float out of her grasp. They fanned out in a large semi-circle on the path in front of her. She leapt off the wall, careful not to step on any of the letters. If they got dirty she would have to start all over again.

'Oh, it's you!' Long legs clad in black pants appeared over the ledge and easily jumped to the ground.

It was the pianist. It's amazing, Nina thought, how a few words spoken in disdain could burn upon your memory so you never forgot the speaker.

'Yes, it is.' There was no way she would give him her full attention. Anyway, it was far more important to gather the letters quickly. It would be even worse if he saw them.

He bent down to help her pick up the sheets of paper but she lunged at him before he had picked up more than a couple.

'I can do it. Thank you.' Still she didn't look at him. She was scraping as much dirt and leaves into the folder as she was paper.

'But you're making a mess.'

'I don't think it's any of your business.'

Out of the corner of her eye, she saw him walk away. He's gone, she thought. In the week since their first exchange she had learnt his name was Nicholas but had managed to look past him in all the classes they shared, even though she felt

58

him watching her. But she kept her head high and avoided his eyes. Now, all her good work had just been undone.

'Here.'

Nina was startled by his voice. She looked up to find him presenting her with some stray letters.

She took them from him and closed the manila folder.

'That must be bit of a drag,' he offered.

She shrugged her shoulders.

'You must get a lot of fan mail.' He waited while she tried to fit the folder into her knapsack. She wasn't doing very well.

'A bit.' Maybe if I answer him he'll leave me alone, she thought. Rather than watching me.

'Look,' he said suddenly, 'most of the time I can be quite a reasonable human being but occasionally I can be a real wanker.'

'And which one are you being today?' She finally shoved the folder in her bag and faced him. She sensed she'd taken him by surprise.

'Is it that difficult to tell?' he laughed.

'What's so funny?' How dare he laugh at her now!

'Well, for a week now I've watched you be super nice to people no matter how they treat you. How come I don't get the super nice Nina too?'

'Because I don't care what you think of me.'

'Why not?'

'Why should I?'

'Because you care what everyone thinks of you.'

'I do not.'

'Yes, you do.'

'I don't have to listen to you criticising me again.' Nina reached for her bag but in her hurry she knocked the contents onto the pavement including, once again, the manila folder.

Nicholas grabbed her arm but she pulled herself free. He held up both his hands to try to show her he meant no harm.

59

'Look,' he spoke quickly, 'I didn't come looking for you to criticise you. I came here to apologise. That's all.'

She threw the empty knapsack onto the footpath with the rest of her things and put her hands on her hips.

'Do you want me to help you pick it all up?'

'I don't want you to help me do anything. Just leave me alone.'

'Okay.'

He waited a moment. But she didn't look at him. The bell rang as she knelt down once again to gather her things. When she looked up, Nicholas was gone.

*

'Could you sign one to Josie and one to Mick.' Nina looked at the tiny bit of paper. She was sure the woman was joking. But she seemed serious so Nina did her best to comply. 'Josie wants to be just like you, but Mick, huh, he'll miss his chance if he doesn't knuckle down and train hard this year.'

'How old are they?' Nina asked as she gave the woman back the now autographed sliver of paper.

'Nine and eleven.'

'Oh, they've got plenty of time then!' Nina told her with a smile.

The woman looked up from the bag in which she had just shoved the paper. 'No such thing anymore. Gotta make the most of what you got. If only I'd had the opportunities kids have today!' She pushed her way back through the crowd. The path the woman made closed quickly. Hundreds of people all eager to have Nina sign their own offerings.

Nina was one of five athletes who had been asked to appear at the opening of Sport Mecca, a new sports superstore in the city. An AFL player, an NFL player, two rowers and Nina were giving the store a bit of gloss and signing a few autographs along the way.

The store was almost ready to close by the time Nina had signed all there was to sign and talked to everyone who wanted a word.

'Thanks for doing that,' said the store manager. He had farewelled the others more than an hour before.

'My pleasure, Steve.' She shook hands with the man. It was nothing more than she was used to these days. And she was being paid very well to do the job. Sam had said that she only had to stay for two hours maximum, but it seemed rude to say that she had to go. So many people would be disappointed.

'Nina, I didn't know if you would still be here!' Alice burst through the revolving entrance to the store. She was lugging her tuba over her shoulder. 'Hi,' she held out her hand to the manager. 'I'm Nina's friend, Alice.' She didn't wait for him to introduce himself. She turned back to Nina. 'I told Nick that I was sure you would be gone but he insisted we see.'

Nina took a moment to register exactly what Alice had said. She looked beyond her friend to see Nicholas coming through the door.

'We couldn't get people away from her,' she heard Steve tell Alice.

'Oh, it's like that everywhere,' said Alice. She often turned up to the public appearances Nina made. 'You've got to have a familiar face somewhere amongst all those crowds,' she would tell Nina. And Alice had a way of pulling the most extraordinary information from people. Often the two of them would be in stitches with things Alice had discovered while Nina had her head down signing autographs.

'Hello, Nina,' said Nicholas as he held out his hand.

She had no choice but to shake it. Nina was beginning to make sense of a conversation a couple of days earlier between her and Alice. Nina had not got the reaction she expected when describing to Alice the lunchtime-letter-signing debacle.

'He's really nice when you get to know him,' Alice had told her.

Nina had been shocked to hear Alice defend him. She was the one person you could usually trust to see through any artifice. 'He's completely full of himself, if you ask me,' she had replied.

'Yeah, but that's what people say about you.'

'But I don't go around making fun of people if they don't know anything about swimming.' Not like Nicholas and his precious classical music, she had thought.

'That's why he wanted to apologise,' Alice had insisted. 'He'd heard the things people say about you and made this lightning judgement based on all of that, rather than finding out for himself. He sort of prides himself on forming his own opinions, I think.'

At that point the bell had rung for the end of lunch and Nina didn't get a chance to quiz Alice further. It hadn't occurred to Nina that they might play in the same band.

'Can we drag her away, now?' Alice asked Steve.

'There's a car waiting to take you home, Nina.'

Nina looked at Alice. 'I was going to catch the bus,' she told Nina. 'What about you, Nick?'

'Same.'

'Could the car wait while we have a coffee, Steve?' Nina asked. She had no idea what she was getting herself into. But she was sure it would be okay if the others were driven home with her.

'Not a problem. It's on level B2 whenever you're ready. I'll tell him you'll be an hour or so.'

'Luxury! I love knowing you, Nina!' Alice linked her arm through Nina's and dragged her out of the store.

'Do you have a favourite place, Nick?' Alice called over her shoulder.

'Yeah, there's a cafe just off the mall,' he told her as he

followed. Outside Sport Mecca Alice pulled Nina aside to let Nicholas pass.

'You lead!'

*

The three of them squeezed Alice's tuba and themselves into a small booth in Nicholas's cafe of choice. Both Alice and Nicholas ordered tea, Nina lemonade, and they agreed to share a large slab of orange-poppyseed cake and ice-cream.

'I didn't think you'd eat that sort of thing,' the waitress said to Nina.

'Best part of doing all that training, isn't it Nina?' Alice said with a grin.

'I'll have to write a letter to the paper. All those articles about how strict you guys are. Making us mortals feel guilty. And it's all crap!' She left the table before Nina had a chance to respond.

Nina looked at her companions. Alice had twisted around in her chair to watch the waitress go back to the kitchen. Nicholas was chuckling to himself as he opened one sugar packet after another and loaded them into his tea. As he emptied each packet he placed them very carefully in front of his cup and saucer until he had six in a row.

'That should really spin her out. In fact we should put them in front of you when we leave, Nina and then she'll really have a story to tell.'

'We can add my four too, Nina.' Alice had turned herself back around to watch Nicholas in action. 'I've never seen anyone have more sugar than me! That's almost disgusting,' she giggled.

'You're just jealous. You stop at four because you think others will find it disgusting. Tell the truth, Alice,' he leaned across the table toward her, waving two full packets in front of her. 'Wouldn't you love to add those extra two packets of sugar.'

Alice squealed with laughter and Nina giggled. She couldn't believe this was the same Nicholas. They had not talked since the last encounter. Year 9 had ended and she hadn't seen him during the school holidays until now. She could not have imagined him as the playful person she saw today teasing Alice. He was almost good-looking when he laughed, she admitted to herself.

Nina didn't have to say much for the rest of the afternoon. Alice and Nicholas told her about the unusual classes they had been to earlier in the day—a series of master classes given by a visiting Russian orchestra. Today's classes were free to any school students who wanted to attend. Alice's attempt at a Russian accent was enough to make the other two give her a hard time while they polished off the cake. They were still laughing when a woman came up to the table with a little girl.

'Excuse me, but we couldn't help noticing you, Nina. Could you sign a napkin for my daughter?'

Nina took the napkin and while signing it had an idea. 'I think you should also get the signatures of my friends.' She looked from Nicholas to Alice, willing them to go with her on this. 'They are international guests of my swimming club and you'll be able to show all your friends their autographs when they win at the next Olympics.' She handed Alice the napkin first. The little girl's eyes grew wide as she took in Alice's generous proportions.

'Eeet vould bee myee pleeezhure,' Alice said in such a strange accent that Nina had to suck on a remaining ice cube from her lemonade to stop herself from laughing.

Nicholas went along with the improvisation but took on a Scottish accent. 'Och, we have been very well looked after in your country!' He finished his signature with a flourish and handed it back to the woman with a little bow of his head.

The woman looked at Nina with a half smile. 'Well, umm,

good luck.' She looked down at her little girl who had not taken her eyes off Alice. 'C'mon dear.' She dragged the girl out the door.

They contained themselves long enough for the autograph hunters to leave the cafe before collapsing on the table in tears of laughter.

HALLET NAMED ATHLETE OF THE YEAR
by Ron Samuels

In a glittering ceremony in the Studio City Banquet Hall, swim queen Nina Hallet was last night named NSW Athlete of the Year.

The award caps off a remarkable twelve months for the Harper Bay teenager who emerged as a major force on the international swimming scene when she won dual gold medals in the 100m and 200m Backstroke at last year's Commonwealth Games in Manchester. She narrowly missed winning gold medals at the Los Angeles World Championships just two weeks later. Since then, she has been unbeaten in every international event in which she has competed, including the World Cup series held during the Australian summer both here and in Europe. Hallet is fast becoming one of our best hopes to win gold for Australia at the Olympic Games in Cape Town next year.

Accepting the award from the Premier, Hallet showed poise beyond her years in spite of the fact that her parents eschew the media training most athletes consider a must if they are to become a marketable commodity. While thanking the team that has assisted her on her meteoric rise, including promising young coach Jack Saunders, she regaled the well-dressed audience with a few stories from the year that has changed her life.

All eyes will be on Hallet in two weeks time at the Australian National Championships at Brisbane's new International Aquatic Centre. Fifty thousand dollars is the prize for the first swimmer to break a world record in the new pool and Hallet is odds-on favourite to walk away with the cash. The Championships will also be the selection trials for the Pan Pacific Championships to be held in Tokyo in August this year.

CHAPTER SEVEN

NINA PEDALLED SLOWLY, following the headland back to Harper Bay. It was a gorgeous Sunday and she was enjoying her bike ride home. She was in no hurry. She had over compensated with the sunscreen so Jack would have no idea of how she had spent her day off. He wouldn't be happy to know that she'd been out in the sun. And he would be furious if he thought she'd ridden her bike all the way to the docks. The Nationals were now just a week away.

'It's imperative to conserve your energy,' he would say over and over again. It was one thing for him to work her hard until the day the swim meet began and still expect best times. But it was quite another for her to risk tiring herself in any other way. Like pedalling a few kilometres on her bike.

'Not that I've got anything to worry about,' Nina said, enjoying the smell of the salty breeze. Jack was just being cautious. The constant travel and racing that Nina had been doing during her school holidays only seemed to be working in her favour. She was powering in the water. Everything was going well. She had never raced so much in her life. And she had swum in cities she had only dreamed about, like Monte Carlo and Barcelona. She was feeling quite invincible.

Anyway she had a good excuse to be on her bike that day—her first practical art project for Year 10. She would miss a week of school for the Nationals and she wanted to get an early start. She had never felt that confident about the practical side of the subject but since she had taken the photos for *sAssy* last year, that had changed. She couldn't use her camera all the time but by taking photos she had started seeing the world through a frame. And that had given her focus. The world didn't seem so completely overwhelming.

Nina continued to take photos as she travelled. She had an agreement with *sAssy* to do a regular 'On the Street' page with fashion looks from teenagers around the world. Or sometimes a Sunday paper would ask her to do a travel story.

But she didn't feel as though she could use any of her travels as inspiration for her project. People at school might think she was a bit stuck-up. And anyway, she had always liked the docks, the juxtaposition—the sheer cliffs of sandstone and the massive container ships—everything so big that even her little body felt it had the power to expand. She had begun her project that morning.

As she got closer to home she was reminded of the other reason to prolong her ride. She had to make a decision about Nicholas. He was playing the piano in a local eisteddfod that afternoon. Not that he had told her.

*

Since that day in the cafe, Nina, Nicholas and Alice had begun to make regular Sunday afternoon trips to the city to see a movie, when Nina was in town. When he had cancelled this Sunday without a reason Nina was disappointed. She had come to rely on Alice and Nicholas. They had changed everything for her at school. When she went back to school for Year 10 she actually had a group to hang with at lunchtime. She was not as comfortable with Nicholas as Alice was. She would never think of calling him Nick. But they had become friends. It had taken Nina a few attempts but he finally admitted to the piano competition.

'Can I come?' she ventured after a moment. They had just finished recess and were on their way to separate classes.

'What for?'

'Why do people usually go? To watch.'

'One watches swimming, one listens to piano.'

'Pedant.' Nina waited for an answer. 'So can I?'

'Don't know why you would want to.'

'You and Alice came to see me at the State Champion-ships.'

'That's different.'

She didn't see why. 'So you don't want me to come?'

It seemed to take forever for him to respond. 'I'm not as good at music as you are at swimming.'

It was not the answer she expected. 'Do I care?' She played safe with one of his favourite lines.

He shrugged. 'No, I don't suppose so.'

'So, I can come?'

'Don't suppose I can stop you.'

'Sometimes getting a straight answer from you is like pull-ing teeth.'

'At least you're not working against a haze of chlorine fumes.'

'You're not funny.'

'Then why are you grinning?'

'Nor original.' When she left him at the corner of the maths building she did the best imitation of flouncing she could muster.

*

Nina pedalled along the esplanade, past the Town Hall, look-ing for somewhere to chain her bike. 'Not that I've decided to go,' she warned herself.

It hadn't occurred to her that he would compare his piano playing to her swimming. Of course, she didn't want to em-barrass him. But she was keen to see him play for real, rather than practise. It was like the difference between watching her train and race, she imagined. And Nicholas had been asking a lot of questions lately. Ever since a man had interrupted their dinner at Pizza Palace one Friday night to ask Nina about visualisation. The man had been introduced to the technique at a business seminar where it was explained that many athletes used it. He was keen to know if Nina 'visualised' with success. When he finally left their table Nicholas had asked her what it was.

'Just this thing where you imagine yourself in your race and you do everything right.' She had dived in for another piece of pizza.

'You imagine yourself winning?'

'Yeah.' He hadn't seemed interested in eating at all. Even though she was still getting to know him, she knew that was unusual. And he never asked about swimming stuff, something she liked about their conversations. 'Isn't this the best pizza?' she'd said, taking another bite.

He hadn't taken the hint. Just sat watching her as though she had a lot more to say. She'd put the pizza down. 'You must do it when you play the piano.'

He had shaken his head. 'Never heard of it.'

She'd given him her best do-you-really-want-to-know-about-this look. But it had had no effect. How could she describe it? 'Well, I see myself at the beginning of the race. I imagine how I'm going to start, you know, getting the best start and getting ahead of everyone. I watch myself making my way down the pool, every stroke, how it feels. I know the time I want to swim for the first fifty metres so I anticipate how my body will be feeling. Like starting to breathe a bit hard but well within myself, comfortable and strong. And then I imagine a killer turn. Like, *pow*! Off the wall leaving everyone behind. And then I can see myself overcoming that really tired feeling I have at the end of the race and surging into the wall really hard.'

When Nina had finished she realised she must've closed her eyes at some point during her speech. She'd opened her eyes in case someone had been watching her and had found Nicholas staring. He was looking at her so intensely it made her blush. She didn't know what to say. 'You know, stuff like that,' was all she could manage.

They had both sat for a moment without saying anything. The silence had made her even more uncomfortable.

'I haven't always been able to imagine winning, of course!' she had laughed.

'You do it before a race then?'

She'd never heard him ask so many questions. 'Umm, it's good before a race. You can imagine yourself not being nervous. You know, so you won't be.' Again she had tried laughing but he'd remained serious. 'But, I think I pretty much do it all the time.'

Nina had managed to steer the conversation away from swimming, and visualising in particular, that night. But in the following weeks, given the slightest opportunity, Nicholas had been back on the subject. He had even telephoned her on the day she got home from the final World Cup in Hobart.

'It's like daydreaming. Only you turn it into something useful,' was the first thing he'd said when she picked up the phone.

'Hi, Nicholas, I'm well thanks, how are you?' she had joked. But he hadn't been deterred.

'I've been trying to force myself to do it and it just wasn't working. But today I was cutting back the camellias and it just happened.'

Nina knew he worked three afternoons a week after school with a local gardening service. But beyond that she had no idea what he was talking about.

'What just happened?'

'Visualising!'

'Oh, yeah.'

Her mother had walked by at that moment. 'Yes,' she'd corrected Nina's grammar. 'Not "yeah".'

'Oh, yes,' she'd tried again. 'I'd better use it to speak properly or Mum will kill me.' She had heard him laugh on the other end.

*

Nina's timing was perfect. It had seemed a waste to ride all the way into town and not hear him play. She'd hardly sat down in the back row of the hall when Nicholas's name was announced and he walked onto the stage. Nina would've loved to stand up and cheer but it didn't seem appropriate. The hall was about half full. The applause was polite. That was the best way she could describe it. So different to what she was used to. Even when there weren't big crowds at the pool there was always a whistle from somewhere, a quick chant from a few team members. She hoped she hadn't done the wrong thing by coming.

But she forgot the thought the moment he started playing. She didn't know the name of the piece but it was familiar, even to her. She realised she'd never really listened to it before. It was beautiful. And romantic, in a sad sort of way. Nina would never have thought the two could go together. She felt as though he was playing it just for her. 'He doesn't even know you're here,' the other voice in her head reminded her.

Nina waited while the rest of the pianists in Nicholas's age group performed. When he was announced the winner she wasn't surprised. Even though she had never seen a competition like this before she knew he was in another class altogether. And the rest of the audience seemed impressed too. When he accepted his ribbon they applauded wildly compared to what she had witnessed earlier.

The presentation was hardly over when she felt a tap on

her shoulder. He motioned her to follow him so she gathered her things and moved as quietly as she could so as not to disturb the next group of performers.

As soon as she was outside he started talking.

'Nina, did you hear that? That was amazing. I mean I don't know if it sounded amazing but it felt amazing. I was possessed or something. I don't normally play like that. I mean, I usually play all right but I was in another place. Or head space. If that makes sense. Brilliant. Not the playing. I mean the feeling.'

'Don't start getting humble now.'

They both laughed. He stopped talking for a moment. They were setting a pretty quick pace along the esplanade. He shook his head.

'Everything just worked. I imagined myself not being nervous, and I wasn't. I imagined just letting go and playing. But I could never imagine playing like that.' He stopped and looked at her for a moment. 'Because I have never played like that!' He threw his hands in the air. He started walking and Nina ran to keep up. Suddenly he was heading to the shops. 'I think we should have an ice-cream to celebrate,' he said, bounding away to Bayside Ice Creamery before she could answer.

He was like a whirlwind. As she followed him she thought of something.

'I got you boysenberry with chocolate. Is that alright?'

She nodded. 'Hey, Nicholas, where are your parents?' She looked back toward the Town Hall, half expecting to find an older couple trying to keep up with their son's suddenly unusual behaviour.

'Not here.' He handed her the double scoop cone and kept walking. 'Do you think we should sit or walk while we eat?'

'Why not?'

He started walking anyway. 'Why not what?

72

'Why aren't your parents here?'

He shrugged his shoulders.

She could see his energy quickly evaporating. She didn't want to spoil his day but she couldn't help herself. 'Don't they come to watch you?'

'No.'

She waited to see if he would go on. But he was concentrating on his ice-cream.

'Why not?'

'Why do you ask so many questions?'

She didn't know what to say. ''Cause I'm a busybody.'

He nodded. Finally he answered her.

'My mother left years ago and my father hates music.'

'Oh.' Just eat your ice-cream, she thought to herself.

'Is that enough for you?'

She nodded. 'Sorry.'

'That's okay.'

'Too bad though, 'cause you were really fantastic.' She hoped she could remind him of the sensations he had been surfing on before she opened her big mouth.

'Better than nice, huh?' he said, reminding her of the way they met.

'Anyone who uses a word like nice to describe playing like that . . . well . . .' She flicked her hand away into the air to indicate nothing in particular at all.

She thought he would laugh but he didn't say anything. He just stopped and stood looking at her. She hadn't noticed how sparkling his eyes were. So blue. She felt flushed and knew she was turning crimson all over. She looked at her ice-cream. It was beginning to melt all over her hand. She looked up to catch him leaning in toward her. His lips brushed her cheek. He smiled. She smiled back. She took a deep breath and they began to walk again. Nina's heart was beating faster than it ever did in any swimming race.

THE SHOCK OF THE NEW

It seems the baton has been well and truly passed to the next generation of super athletes — they're young, they're talented and they have no respect for their elders!

This month *Sports International* makes some forward predictions.

From the golden beaches of sunny Sydney to the mountains of Marrakech — when you watch these athletes win Olympic gold medals next year, remember you read it here first!

In Australia, they have a new 'It' girl. Many say they have never seen anything like her. And for a country that has produced as many swimming golden girls as this one, that's saying something. This new water-baby goes by the name of Nina Hallet. She shimmies, slides and rolls through the water in a way that would make her predecessors proud. And to paraphrase something once said of another great gal, 'she does it backwards'.

Less than a year ago no one had ever heard of Nina Hallet. Not anyone who mattered anyway. But at the Los Angeles World Championships she frightened the wits out of our own reigning world record holder and Olympic champion, Rain Summers. Luckily Rain had declared the Worlds would be her last international meet before she retired to enjoy marital bliss. Otherwise her departure might be mistaken for running for cover.

Of course, there was always the chance that it was just a fluke. Professional sport is littered with stories of the next great hope. The unlucky group who catch a ride on hard work and hormones converging at just the right time but are never heard of again.

But not this dynamo. Last month she was back at the Australian National Championships, leaving everyone in her wake as she won her races oh so close to the world records Rain has left behind.

The fastest in the world this year. No resting, no shaving. She's saving that for the Pan Pacific Championships in two months time. Will she predict how fast she can go?

'I wouldn't want to put a limit on myself like that,' she answers with a smile. But beware — she can't even sit still when she speaks!

CHAPTER EIGHT

NINA STOOD ON one of the long benches clapping as loudly as she could. Gradually the small gathering started chanting, 'Jake, Jake, Jake' over and over, faster and faster, which delighted the young man who was the centre of attention.

Jake confidently took the microphone from Richard Benson, the head coach of the Aquanauts organisation. The organisation now had two Australian representatives within its ranks and to celebrate were holding a Saturday morning, post-training breakfast barbecue.

Nina was exhausted after a month of cramming international TV and magazine interviews into her normal schedule. Sam had promised her it would all end this week and she'd been looking forward to an afternoon of doing nothing.

But Jake had made the Australian team and was to accompany her to the Pan Pacific Championships in Tokyo. His feet were yet to hit the ground. Nina remembered the feeling and she was determined to share it with him. Even if she couldn't eat anything just yet. She still had to run the six kilometres home before she could eat and really relax.

'Thanks, Mr Benson, it was good of you to come to our little party.'

Nina wasn't the only one who caught the irony in Jake's words. The organisation had three bases across the city. While they all came under the one club banner there was as much competition within the club as there was between other clubs. Swimmers and parents alike were loyal to their particular coach and his or her methods. Richard Benson was head coach in name only. For him to appear when there was glory to bask in was seen as pretty typical.

'I have a few people to thank,' Jake continued. 'Jack, my main man, who keeps persisting with me. And my mum who does the same, only on a grander scale. And . . .' Jake's chest puffed like a peacock's, his head bobbing as if trying move into its new, elevated position, '. . . my Aquanauts and Australian team mate—I can't get used to saying that so I'll say it again, just in case you didn't get it—my Australian team mate, Nina.'

Everyone laughed and clapped again. Tears rolled down Jake's mother's face as Nina's mum put an arm around her shoulder and hugged her.

'Because, you know, she was out there before any of us, showing it was possible for people like us to do stuff like this. Where are you anyway?' When Jake spotted her up on the bench he signalled her down. 'Get over here, Nina.'

At that point Mr Benson took the microphone. 'Let's wish Nina and Jake all the best on their Pan Pac campaigns!'

He raised his glass of orange juice and the group followed his example.

*

It was only the thought that this was the last bit of exercise she had to do for the rest of the weekend that kept her running all the way home. Her brother was heading off on his skateboard as she ran up the final hill to the house. He acknowledged her as he passed but was moving too quickly for her to find out where he was going. The weather was still great so she presumed he was heading to the beach.

Nina had showered and was eating scrambled eggs by the time her mother returned home. After the barbecue, Annette Hallet had gone on to her Saturday morning ritual of coffee with Nina's aunt at The Chat Room. The cafe was their favourite and they often talked of Andy, the young man who owned the place. It seemed he showered them with attention and it made their day. She was always in a good mood and full of gossip when Auntie Ray dropped her back at the house.

Nina was reading *Lord of the Flies*, preparing for an essay she had to write, when her mother walked in.

'Nina, is your Nicholas, Nicholas Coulter?'

'He's not my Nicholas,' she answered without looking up from the book. She needed to show her mum that she didn't have time to talk.

But rather than unpacking the shopping, she stood looking at Nina, saying nothing. Nina gave in and looked up at her.

'I just thought you might be interested to know that Nicholas is in hospital,' said her mum.

*

Nina walked along the hospital corridor looking for ward 11C. The nurse had pointed her in this direction and Nina hadn't waited for further instructions. She seemed to be swamped with a million other requests and enquiries.

A phone call to the hospital on Saturday afternoon had found Nina talking to Mr Coulter. She introduced herself, not knowing if he knew anything of her friendship with his son. But as soon as she said her name he told her everything that had happened. Excruciating stomach pains on Thursday night, a rushed trip to the hospital and an emergency operation to remove an exploding appendix was the reason Nicholas had been a no-show at school on Friday. Nina asked if she could visit when he came home but Mr Coulter told her to come to the hospital.

'I'll drive you home when visiting hours are finished,' he volunteered. 'He gets sick of seeing my ugly mug,' was his explanation.

The big yellow door to the ward was closed. She looked down at the presents she held. The book, she knew, was a good choice. But she was unsure about the flowers. They were only daisies but she wondered if they were a bit much. They were just meant to be cheery.

'They don't mean anything more than that,' she told herself. 'Really?' came another voice from somewhere in her head.

She poked her head around the door. Pale yellow curtains completely surrounded the first bed. From the instructions that were coming from behind the curtains, someone was obviously performing a check-up.

There was a man leaning on the end of the bed closer to the window. He had the same lanky build as her friend. As soon as he saw Nina he moved toward her.

'Mr Coulter?'

'Hi, Nina,' Mr Coulter said in an exaggerated whisper. 'Thanks for coming.' He led her to the bed where Nicholas lay sleeping.

'How is he?' Nina asked.

'Not too bad, although his timing is lousy,' Mr Coulter joked, indicating his sleeping son. 'He dozed off after lunch, apparently, and I don't like to wake him.'

Nina smiled but she didn't have a clue what to say to him. The least Nicholas could do was wake up. She remembered her presents.

'Oh, I brought these.'

'Great. Well, I'll make myself useful and see if I can find a vase for them.' Mr Coulter took the flowers. 'Sit over by the bed. Once I'm out of the room he'll probably wake up.'

Nina sat down and looked at her sleeping friend. There were no real signs of the operation he had just been through. She looked at his eyes. Her mother often asked her how she was feeling just because of the black rings she claimed to be

78

under Nina's eyes. Occasionally Nina would check in the mirror to see if her eyes were black enough to convince her mother she needed a day off school. There were dark smudges under Nicholas's eyes. Suddenly she realised she was staring at him. What if he should wake up, or his father return?

She sat back in her chair and looked around. Beside the bed she found a magazine, which she began to flick through before a sleepy voice interrupted her.

'How long have you been here?'

'Not long.' She closed the magazine and leant closer to the bed in case the effort to speak wore him out. Your dad is outside looking for a vase.'

Nicholas just nodded and smiled. His eyes blinked a few times as he struggled to wake up. His father appeared from around the curtain with a small glass vase that held the bedraggled daisies.

'Best I could do,' he told Nina. He was on his way around to the side of the bed when she indicated with a nod of her head that Nicholas was awake. It seemed to stop him from moving closer. There was a moment of silence.

'Hi, mate.'

'Hi, Dad.'

Mr Coulter remembered what he held in his hands. 'Nina brought you some flowers.'

Nicholas looked at Nina. 'Thank you.' He made an attempt to sit up in his bed but it was a painful manoeuvre. Nina jumped up as Mr Coulter moved in.

'I can help.' He handed the flowers to Nina.

'I'm okay,' Nicholas protested but Mr Coulter gently lifted him under the shoulders as Nina put the daisies on the bed-side table and arranged the pillows in a more comfortable place for Nicholas.

'Is that better?' It was a tentative inquiry.

'Thanks,' Nicholas acknowledged the help.

Nina had the feeling it was going to be a long afternoon.

'Nicholas has seen enough of me over the last couple of days, haven't you, mate?' Mr Coulter had started gathering his things and didn't wait for his son to answer. 'I'm sure you guys can talk a lot easier without me here. Visiting hours are nearly over so I'll wait in the tea room down the hall, Nina.'

'No, really, Mr Coulter, I don't want to interrupt you . . .' A few moments ago she would have jumped at the chance of being alone with Nicholas but now it made her nervous.

But Nicholas's father was on his way. 'There's no rush. I'll see you tomorrow, mate.'

Nina watched Mr Coulter walk out the door before turning to Nicholas. 'Did I do something wrong?'

Nicholas made an attempt at a laugh but the strain on his stomach muscles left his face awash with pain.

'No, Nina,' he said when he had recovered. 'That's just me and my dad!'

*

If Nina were sitting in the car with her own father they would have been singing loudly to the song on the radio. They spent so much time together travelling to workouts or swim meets and listening to radio stations that played greatest-memories-type music that Nina knew all the words to many of the songs. And whether she liked the music or not didn't matter because Nina and her dad had the best time singing together.

But this car was different. The radio volume was low which meant there was no need to raise your voice at all. In Nina's family, music was heard at two volumes—loud or very loud. And conversation was pretty much the same. Nina laughed to herself at the thought.

'Something funny?'

She didn't realise she had laughed out loud.

'Oh, just thinking.'

Mr Coulter nodded. 'It was good of you to visit Nicholas. He talks about you a lot.'

'He does?'

'You sound surprised.'

Nicholas had never talked about his father before she forced the conversation at the eisteddfod so she had presumed he didn't talk to his father about her. 'Well, you know Nicholas, he isn't exactly a chatterbox.'

Mr Coulter smiled. 'That's true.'

Another song that she knew came on the radio. She started humming it to herself.

'You can turn it up if you like.'

'Oh no, I know you don't like music.' She had blurted it out before she realised what she'd said.

'I don't like music?' Mr Coulter slammed the brakes on hard and a horn blared. As the car behind swerved to avoid them the driver shouted expletives and Mr Coulter responded with a few of his own.

'Sorry,' he said to Nina. 'Are you all right?'

She nodded.

He started to accelerate again. 'Did Nicholas tell you I don't like music?'

She hesitated before answering. Was there any way she could avoid having this conversation, she wondered. The only reassuring thing was that they were not far from her home. She nodded again.

Mr Coulter didn't say anything. Nina looked at him from out of the corner of her eye. He looked dejected.

'Look, it was my fault,' she volunteered. 'I went to see him play at that last eisteddfod and I hassled him about where his parents were and—to make me shut up, probably—he said that you didn't like music.' She knew it was a messy explanation but it was the best she could do.

'What did he say about his mother?'

'Just that she had gone.'

Mr Coulter nodded slowly as he turned the corner. One to go, Nina thought, and then we will be in my street. She couldn't wait to get out of the car.

Nothing was said until Nina pointed to the house she lived in. As she opened the car door, he finally spoke.

'You know, his mother said I loved music more than her.' Mr Coulter was looking ahead, through the car windscreen. 'It's funny, isn't it?' But when he turned to Nina he didn't look amused.

She had no idea what he was talking about and she didn't want to hang around to find out. 'Thanks for the lift, Mr Coulter.' It was the only thing she could think of to say.

'Yeah, sure Nina,' he answered as if he hadn't really heard.

She waited on the curb until he drove off, trying to imagine what it must be like to live in a house with Nicholas and his dad. She wondered if they ever really spoke to one another. Nina took a deep breath. She could smell the roast her mum was cooking for dinner. And there was an essay to finish before she ate. She wondered how much time she had.

CHAPTER NINE

NINA FELT ABOUT ten feet tall as she jumped out of the bus and followed the rest of the Australian team through a couple of winding corridors and into the massive auditorium.

From the moment she had first walked onto the pool deck in Tokyo, just over a week ago, she loved the facility. It had been built for an Olympic games well before Nina was born and she couldn't help wonder what it must have been like for the swimmers all those years ago. There had been many impressive pools built since then, but this one had stood the test of time—a perfect venue for the Pan Pacific Championships. The spiralling height of the building made the pool seem so little, much shorter than the fifty metres it was supposed to be. And fast.

'Hey, Nina.'

The American coach, Dennis Paul, interrupted her thoughts as she walked past him. He already had his athletes in the pool warming up.

'How are you, Coach Paul?'

'Looking forward to seeing you swim, that's for sure.'

'Thanks,' she answered as she continued walking. Not as much as I am, she thought to herself. Since the retirement of Rain Summers after the World Championships, the Americans were yet to produce another backstroker of her calibre. At least not one that had shown themselves. Nina had qualified for the final of the 100m Backstroke that night and while she wasn't about to take anyone for granted, she just knew she wouldn't be beaten tonight.

'Another one of your fans?'

Jake had dropped back to join her. She smiled without saying anything. She didn't feel much like talking tonight. Even to Jake. He had been like a wide-eyed puppy on the trip so far, astonished by the mad, chaotic delights of Tokyo and, it seemed, completely in awe of his old friend. So many times Nina would look up to find him looking at her, shaking his head.

'What?' she would ask.

'It's like it's not even you, Nina. You're so grown up.' Or sometimes he would say, 'How did you get to know all these things?'

Quite a few times he had said, 'that's not how we do it at home' until Nina had suggested it would be a shame to come such a long way and find everything was the same. Jake had stopped saying it after that.

He matched her stride as they walked along the deck.

'How are you feeling?'

'Good,' she said emphatically.

'So do you reckon it's on?'

She laughed. She knew he was talking about a world record. That's all everyone talked about, but it was never actually stated.

'I reckon it might be.'

But she wasn't going to say any more than that. Since that night at the Commonwealth Games trials, when she had kept to herself exactly how she felt, she had created a new superstition for herself. 'Good' was a poor description but any further elaboration might destroy the mystery. And it *was* a mystery. Before she wound down her training for this competition, she wondered if she would ever feel that weightlessness again. That rush of water as it slipped by like quicksilver. She had become more accustomed to it feeling like molasses as she ploughed through it during long, hard training sets.

But on the second night, when they had come for a work-out in the Tokyo pool, she had dived in and, like magic, there it was. She was so thrilled with her discovery that she broke out of the freestyle she was swimming and began diving like a dolphin. She laughed out loud under the water as her body rolled and undulated along the bottom of the pool before she re-surfaced and resumed the more traditional stroke.

Maybe there was something in the messages Jake had been giving her on this trip. Until he pointed it out, she didn't feel any different to the person she was when this had all begun. But being in Tokyo at the Pan Pacific Championships, with most of the world to swim against, she was comfortable. More than comfortable. It was her place. She belonged here. And she knew exactly what she was doing.

'They want me to go back to the hotel after I've swum through the warm-up, to rest for the 200m Breaststroke to-morrow. But I want to see you swim.'

'Oh,' Nina focused her attention on Jake again. For all her experience, she knew she wanted Jake to be by the pool when she swam tonight, just as her mum and dad would be some-where in the grandstand. The money Nina had earned over the last year was much more than she needed to buy them tickets and accommodation in Tokyo to see her swim. Her gift had caused great excitement in the Hallet household.

'Don't worry,' Jake moved in close to her as if he was about to divulge state secrets. 'I'll do my best not to be noticed. Brian will forget where I am once the swimming has started.'

Nina nodded in agreement. Brian Cook, the head coach, often told swimmers to go back to the hotel early to rest up for their own events. But the excitement of the night's events would mean that, just as often, he would forget his own in-structions until much later. Nina was often on the receiving end of a frustrated stare from him because she hated to leave the atmosphere of the pool and the events.

'Don't get yourself in trouble for me, Jake,' she cautioned.

'Don't know anyone I would rather get in trouble for, Nina.'

*

By the time Nina was introduced to the crowd from her position in lane four, she had all but shut out the rest of the world. It was not a conscious thing. It was just that, as the evening moved toward her race, the 100m Backstroke, her body was in full volume and everything beyond it was turned down.

As she peeled off her green tracksuit she was aware of feeling really warm, almost clammy. Her body felt heavy, cumbersome.

'Nerves,' she said to herself, 'nothing more.' It wasn't the first time she was glad her race started in the water. She didn't have to pretend to false start or whatever it was the others had to do to get wet.

The whistle blew and she moved to the pool. She stood for a moment behind her lane and took a quick glance up to where her parents were sitting. So high up in the stands but as clear to her as if they were a metre away. Her father had one arm around her mother's shoulders and the other he raised in the air in a giant wave. She gave a small wave back, keeping it by the side of her body, in acknowledgment. Then she jumped into the water. Used the blocks to pull herself up into the crouched position. And when the gun went, away she flew.

For months she had been working hard at turning her stomach muscles into rocks. They would give her power to execute a series of mighty underwater butterfly kicks off the starting block. She had imagined, again and again, the flick of her feet causing an unstoppable momentum that would bring her back to the surface so far in front of the others that they would know right then that the race was hers alone.

As her arms caught up with the rest of her body, she made a quick check of her competition. Jebby was the only

Australian in the race and Nina had long ago stopped worrying about her. Nor was there anyone else of real note—they were all about level with her knees. Yes, so far so good.

She brought her concentration back to herself, checking that her body was rotating along the invisible line that ran through the centre of her body, her stroke as long as she could make it. She felt good. It's only the first fifty, a voice cautioned, so not so fast. Take it steady.

But Nina had never had such difficulty holding herself back. Her arms wanted to spin. She checked her breath. It was steady. There didn't seem to be too much effort involved. She made a decision. Spin away ninja, your body seems to be handling it, she told herself.

The flags came up and led her into the turn. Again the big flutter kick under the water. Now she didn't worry about letting herself go. She grabbed hold of the water, making sure every handful did the work it was supposed to do. There was no one to challenge her down the second lap. If she were to swim her way to a world record she would have to do it alone.

The screaming came from nowhere. What was it, her limbs, her body demanding relief? Had she gone too hard too early and worn herself out with the effort? Jack would kill her. She would kill herself! 'Concentrate,' she told herself, 'where is the screaming coming from?' It definitely wasn't from within. She was relieved.

But from where? Outside her perhaps. And then she realised—it was the crowd, of course! They were cheering for her. She could hear the pool announcer stirring them along. She must be on target. She would use their momentum to bring her into the wall.

Her muscles were beginning to moan. She pushed herself harder. Her body began to feel weak. Fifteen metres, twelve metres, the flags must come soon, she thought. Then, there they were and she knew she had only four strokes to go. She pushed her hand into the finish as firmly as she could before sinking below the surface as her body was released from its service.

When she resurfaced the stands were on their feet. Nina reached for the lane rope for support while her lungs sucked in the air they craved. She was aware of the other girls finishing. She saw her mum and dad jumping up and down and going crazy. She could see Jake and Dominic giving one another a hug, while the rest of the Australian team chanted and whistled and punched the air.

The announcer was repeating over and over again the words Nina had dreamed she would hear. She looked to the scoreboard. There it was. Two little letters beside her name: WR. They confirmed this whole crazy scene, as Jake would surely describe it.

'World record,' she whispered to herself, and the words brought a flood of exhilaration. She felt a tightness in her chest, a ball of something rising up into her throat and tickling her mouth until it burst forth to become an uncontrollable grin. And then a laugh.

But this was a feeling beyond happiness. It was something more. She felt complete. While everyone danced and roared and fussed around her, she knew that this effort was hers. It was the result of a secret pact between her mind and her body that one day she would stand up and give the world a measure of everything she tried to be.

As she pulled herself out of the water, stood by the side of the pool and lifted both her arms up to acknowledge the applause of the crowd, she felt sure that nobody would ever be able to take that away from her.

*

Nina sat in the middle of the eight Australians who had broken world records at the Pan Pacific Championships. This was the first press conference given by the Australian team on their arrival back in the country. And while Nina was used to seeing a sea of journalists and cameramen in front of her, the crowd this morning was more on the scale of an ocean.

The swimmers had been taken straight to a city hotel when they had landed a couple of hours earlier, to shower and change before they faced the press in the hotel convention room. Nina had been given a lavish suite filled with flowers, fruit and chocolate. When her mother had arrived with fresh clothes for Nina to wear they had tried every chair and sofa in the three rooms to see which had the best view of the harbour, which was so conveniently laid out before them. She had even had a bath just to see what it was like to watch the ferries come into the Quay while she was surrounded by bubbles. While Nina soaked her mum relaxed on the chaise longue in the corner of the bathroom. Nina had a box of chocolates perched on the end of the bath and was drinking orange juice while her mother sipped on champagne.

'I feel like a queen, Nina, and I haven't even done any-thing!' Her mum stretched like a cat in the warm sun. 'I'm glad I won't be near any reporters. One glass of champagne and already I'm a giggling mess.'

When Ace Quinn arrived to do Nina's hair and make-up, Nina's mother made him sit down and join her for a glass of champagne before he began his work.

'Who'd have thought when I was first called in to work on this little Raggedy Ann that we'd be sitting here in such luxury,' he declared as he poured himself another drink.

Back in the convention room, Nina began to understand exactly what the Australian swimming team had achieved. In Tokyo they were told they were the most successful team for almost thirty years. But Nina had not understood the ramifi-cations of that. It wasn't the achievements in Tokyo that were being celebrated so much as the anticipated achievements in twelve months time at the Olympic Games.

'I feel like a rock star,' she whispered to Dominic who was seated beside her.

'Cool, isn't it? I think this colour is very becoming, don't you?' he indicated the massive backdrop they sat in front of. The golden fabric highlighted not just their medals, but the name of the hotel chain that was playing host today.

'There's our Mr Johnson, right on time.'

Nina saw Sam standing against the wall behind the press. He raised his hand and formed the okay sign with his hands.

'Always checking up on us,' Dominic said. He put his hands around Nina's throat and pretended to strangle her. 'No, Sam, I really want to throttle this one because she's taking all the attention away from me!'

But he was only speaking loud enough for Nina to hear him. She was forced to jab Dominic in the ribs before he would let go. She righted herself in time to see Sam laughing at them.

'I don't know why I put up with you,' she said as she pretended to straighten her clothes and pat her hair back into an imaginary style. 'I'm trying to behave like a *dual* world record holder, if you don't mind.' Nina had broken world records in both the 100m and 200m Backstroke in Tokyo. Whereas Dominic, while breaking his own world record in the 200m Individual Medley in Tokyo, only held one.

'Come and talk to me when you back up and break them again and again, huh!'

'Don't worry, I will,' she countered as the general manager of the hotel moved forward to get the press conference under way. Dominic raised his eyebrows as if to say 'here we go'.

Nina was glad she was sitting next to Dominic. One of the better things about breaking her world records in Tokyo was that it made her feel as though she had the right to be sitting next to him. Not that he was the kind of person to make her feel otherwise. He had been so generous with his friendship and advice from the moment she had first made the Australian team. He always spoke to her as though being the best in the world was never in doubt. It felt good to live up to his high opinion of her.

'You must be on cloud nine, Nina?' The question brought her back to the convention room.

'More like cloud five thousand and nine, Sally.' Nina had spotted the ABC reporter before the conference began. 'Jack and I have trained and talked about this for more than a year now and to finally see it come to fruition was very satisfying.'

'Will you go with him when he moves?' The question came from beyond the bank of TV cameras. It wasn't a familiar voice.

'Pardon?' Nina tried to determine who had asked the question. She was sure she had not heard correctly.

'Rick Jeffries from the *Melbourne Monitor*. I was wondering if you will move with Jack when he goes to the Water Knights?'

The Water Knights was a Melbourne club, Nina knew that, but she didn't know what they had to do with Jack.

'Umm, I'm sorry,' she looked at Dominic and grabbed for the glass of water. 'I don't think that's something we have to worry about until after the Olympics.' She laughed to emphasise how seriously she took the question. Dominic laughed with her. They both sounded hollow, she thought. When there was no response she continued. 'Is it?'

Everyone turned to see if Rick Jeffries would provide an explanation.

'I'm sorry, Nina, I thought you would know,' Rick said. 'I understand that Jack has agreed to coach the Water Knights from September.'

Nina's mouth was dry. Next month. She couldn't believe what she was hearing. Jack had sent her congratulatory telegrams when she was in Tokyo but he hadn't mentioned anything else. When was he going to tell her, she wondered. She tried to take a sip of water but missed her mouth and spilt it down the front of her sweatshirt. She vainly tried to wipe the wet area. Dominic took the glass from her and put his arm around her shoulders.

'Are you all right?' she heard him ask.

She nodded. She knew that every camera was trained on her at this very minute. Why was Jack leaving? Was it something she had done? She was going to have to get herself together and finish the conference and then get an explanation. But leaving her now—with the Olympics a year away. She thought of Jake. Jack was like a father to Jake. He would be devastated.'

'Don't think about that now,' she told herself.

She lifted her head. She sat up and shook off Dominic's arm. It was not the time to indulge in sympathy.

'I'm sorry. I didn't know Jack was leaving.' She swallowed hard. What to say, how to be diplomatic? 'Obviously, I wish him well.' She shrugged her shoulders. 'I don't know any of the details so all I can really say is good luck to him.' She gave her best impression of a smile. Was that enough, she wondered? Did she have to say anymore?

The room erupted in questions all at once. Sam came from nowhere and stood in front of Nina, holding up his arms.

'Ladies and gentlemen, obviously you have surprised Nina this morning, all of us in fact,' he turned to Nina as he spoke, indicating that this was news to him too. 'If you could confine your questions to the Pan Pacs and the tremendous performances of the team, that would be appreciated. As you can see, Nina can't add anything more to the news that her coach is apparently changing clubs because she didn't know herself. We will make a statement about that later today. Okay?'

He turned back to Nina. 'Okay, Nina?'

She nodded. The Pan Pacs. She couldn't even remember

the Pan Pacs. The press conference continued. She was aware of Dominic holding her hand under the table. Questions were politely asked and politely answered. When it ended there were more presentations, more photographs, more flowers, more platitudes. She was aware of her mother hovering, Sam on his mobile phone. Finally she was released to ask a few questions of her own.

*

The only noise in the room was the sound of Jake's sobs.

Jack sat in the opposite corner to Jake, on top of his now empty desk, both hands gripping the edge, his head hanging.

But Nina couldn't sit. And she had no intention of letting him see her cry. She had stood next to Jake while Jack had given them his explanation. More money. Head coaching position. A chance he would never have within the Aquanauts organisation. Maybe a chance as an Australian team coach. And his girlfriend was from Melbourne. She wanted to go home.

They could join him if they wanted, he added. The Water Knights would make sure they were both well looked after. He hoped they both understood. Nina found herself nodding as he spoke. They were all reasonable excuses. All perfectly logical.

'Hey, guys, you know this is a difficult decision for me too.'

When his eyes began to well with tears, Nina had to move. She couldn't bear to look at him. She walked around the room. She felt like her temples would burst she was so angry. Her jaw was hurting from clenching it so hard. She had a pain in her stomach.

How she wanted to speak! To say, how could you? How dare you? How could you leave me when I have given you the reputation you now have? *I* am the reason you were offered this new job. *I* have given your stupid girlfriend the

93

opportunity to go back to her precious home. One more year and you could coach anywhere in the world if you wanted to.

But she said nothing. She looked out the window to where her mother and Mrs Watson stood near their parked cars. Her mother with her arms locked across her chest. Mrs Watson pacing back and forth.

It had been the only thing their mothers had talked about since the press conference that morning. Their opinions swung wildly from outrage to understanding. From disbelief to disgust. They had assumed they were all on this journey together. For one of the key players to get off now and abandon their children was incomprehensible to them. *They* had lived up to their part of the bargain.

Nina and Jake had not said much. And Nina knew, as she stood looking at the older women, she would not say anything now. She was ashamed of her earlier thoughts. She was disappointed. But Jack had a right to decide what to do with his life. Who was she to make demands? He was free to go. She should not be so conceited. Or selfish. She had never been a sore loser and she would not be one now.

She turned away from the window and went back to Jake. She squeezed his shoulder for reassurance. There was nothing more to say. Anyway, it was time for Jack to get back on the pool deck for his final training session. She and Jake would not swim tonight. They deserved a week of rest after the Pan Pacs. The new coach would be at the pool when they returned.

She walked over to her former coach and held her hand out to shake his. He looked up, pushed himself off the desk.

'I've got something for you both.'

From the drawer he pulled out two exquisitely wrapped tiny boxes. Nina looked at Jake. He could determine whether to open it now in front of Jack. He didn't hesitate so Nina did the same. A watch for Jake and a pair of diamond earrings for Nina.

Jake gave Jack a hug. His thank you was genuine, Nina thought. She held out her hand again and Jack shook it with both of his. He knew better than to try for a hug from her.

'You know, you can always call me, Nina, if you need anything.'

She nodded. 'Good luck, Jack.'

She turned and let Jake lead her through the door to the foyer and out to the car park. As she had done a million times before, she walked past the garbage bin at the entrance to the pool and, without looking, dropped whatever was in her hand into the bin. Usually it was a gum wrapper. She continued on to the car.

'Talk to you tomorrow?' she called to Jake as they got into their respective vehicles.

Her mother spoke softly as Nina climbed into the car. 'What did you throw in the bin, Neen?'

Nina slid her seatbelt across her body and locked it into place. 'Nothing.'

She would have been fine if she'd just looked straight ahead and not at her mum. But it was those big dark eyes, full of pain and pride, that finally brought her undone.

CHAPTER TEN

NINA DIDN'T KNOW if it was the ringing of the phone that woke her up, or her mum talking to whoever was on the other end. She did know that she was awake by the time her mother hung up. Nina heard her pull a chair out from under the dining room table and sit down. The television was not on. She imagined her father sitting at the table doing the crossword from the day's paper and her mother reading her latest book.

Nina sat up, thirsty. A glass of water might help her get back to sleep. She was about to get out of bed when her father started talking.

'Was that Sam?'

There was no answer from her mother. But the fragments of conversation Nina had overheard when her mother was on the phone now made sense. They had all met with Sam the day before. None of them had imagined the effect a couple of world records might have. Maybe Sam had. But not Nina or her mother and father. They had sat in silence while Sam led them through the twenty or more offers made to Nina. There were the obvious ones; sportswear, sporting goods, sport-related products like cosmetics and other personal grooming items. White goods, brown goods, a furniture warehouse. A fashion label. The list went on and on.

Sam said it was a matter of choosing the right product or combination of products. Make the most of everything on offer, without overkill. And choose products Nina could feel strongly about.

If the volume of requests was daunting for the Hallets, the amount of money on offer was almost terrifying. And Sam thought he could get more! Many of the deals included fat monetary incentives for Nina to win gold medals at the Olympic Games. The world records Nina had broken in Tokyo would make her a wealthy girl. Winning gold medals at the Games in a year's time would make her a *very* wealthy girl. But there was a lot of training to do between now and then. And there would be commitments, out of the pool, to the companies she was about to become associated with. Which didn't leave a lot of time for school.

Nina heard her mother finally speak.

'You think I am wrong, don't you?'

'I don't think you're wrong, Annette.'

'But you don't think it's important that she keeps going to school.'

There was a pause.

'I just don't feel as strongly about it as you do.'

'You think we should let her give up her education and just swim.'

'Nobody said she should give up her education.'

'Same thing.'

'No it isn't. She could go back to school after the Olympics.'

'After she has won a gold medal at the Olympics and earned millions of dollars do you really think she will go back to school?'

'She wouldn't have to, would she?' Her father gave a half laugh. Her mother didn't join in. Silence again.

'You think this is funny.'

'Oh, Annette, c'mon.'

'Don't "c'mon" me!'

Nina held her breath to see which way the conversation would go. She couldn't remember the last time her parents had argued.

'Sweetheart, it's just not a position I have ever been in before. I'm trying to see the positive side of my daughter being offered hundreds and thousands of dollars, which will become millions of dollars if she wins two Olympic gold medals next year—which she has a good chance of doing because she happens to hold two world records right now and is the fastest in the world at what she does.'

'And she has done that while being at school.'

'Yes, I know that.'

'You don't think it's putting too much pressure on her to take her out of school? It's putting all her eggs in one basket. At least if she is at school she will have a distraction.'

She heard her father sigh and the wooden chair creak.

'She doesn't even have to worry about doing all that well at school,' her mother continued. 'It will just give her something else to think about. She'll have something else to talk about at the promotions she has to attend.'

'They don't want her to talk about anything other than her swimming.'

'She's popular because she has a character that isn't one dimensional.'

'Oh, get real, Annette. She's popular because she is the best in the world at sport and Australians love sport. Just because you don't happen to agree with that part of the Australian psyche doesn't mean you should go around undermining it. Nothing else will ever be as important to the majority of Australians as how well Nina does next year. That is what we have to understand and find a way of helping her with it. Yes, she can go to school but it's a minor detail. Whether she is smart and wins or stupid and wins doesn't matter—as long as she wins.'

'I can't believe I am hearing you speak like this. I can't believe you think like this. I can't believe you could call school a minor detail. And what if she doesn't win?'

Nina knew her mother was getting frustrated. Her voice was getting higher and she was speaking faster.

'Answer me that, Geoff. She will have nothing. Not even school. All she will be qualified to do is be a swimming coach. And she will be a failure to her father who only wants her to be a gold medallist.'

'She will not be a failure to me if she doesn't win. But she will be a failure to you even if she wins because that won't be enough for you. She has to be a bloody brilliant scholar too. Just because that is what your father expected from you. For anyone else it would be enough to be brilliant at one thing. But not for you. Nothing she ever does will ever be enough for you.'

'How dare you say that!'

'Tell me the truth, Annette. Knowing Nina, do you really think she could go into Year 11 and take it easy? Not worry about her exams or her results? Just treat it as a distraction? Especially when she knows how important it is to you?'

Nina couldn't hear her mother's answer. She heard her father get out of his chair.

'Please don't cry, Annette.' There were another few moments before she heard her father speak again. 'I'm sorry, love.'

'You think I'm being ridiculous about this, don't you?' She could hear her mother trying to speak through tears. Nina hoped her father was giving her a hug.

'I think you are trying to protect our little girl.' His voice was reassuring.

'You didn't answer my question though.'

Her father gave another half laugh before answering. 'Only in the nicest possible way.'

Nina lay back on her pillow and pulled the doona up around her chin. She had forgotten about her thirst. She just hoped her mum and dad were okay.

*

Nina's first thought was what a coincidence that her cousin, who lived on the other side of the city, was dining at the same restaurant. She was about to call back to her mum and say 'look who's here,' when her eye caught sight of someone else she knew. Elkie Rogers, whom Nina had swum against when they were both little, was at another table. Elkie played netball now and had just made the State squad for the next National Championships. Nina spoke to Elkie on the phone more than she saw her these days.

And then she saw Jake, and some of the other squad members—Tom Watson, Angel Murphy and Gillian Quick. And there was Nicholas and Alice, sitting with Allan Sanders who sometimes joined them at lunch, and Rose Mayer—who started at Harper in Year 10 and had gradually become friends with Nina's little group.

Even the twins, Jacqui and Georgia, who lived next door to Nina but went to a private school in the city, were there.

What should have been obvious took a relatively long time to sink in. As she looked around she realised she knew everyone in the local Italian restaurant. But she didn't put it all together until they all jumped up and yelled.

'Surprise!'

She turned to her mother and father for some explanation but they just smiled and shrugged their shoulders. Everyone was thrilled that they had kept the congratulatory dinner a secret.

'I knew I just had to stay away from you, Nina,' Alice told her. 'I told Nick I would kill myself if I opened my big mouth!'

'I told her she wouldn't have to because I would do it for her,' Nicholas interrupted but he couldn't stop Alice from finishing her tale.

'And even worse than telling you, I worried that I would accidentally let Shan and those girls know about it—and they would tell you! Oh, it's been such a stressful week, Nina. I hope you don't break world records too often. I don't think I can cope.' With that Alice flopped back in her chair and held her hand to her head like an overdramatic silent film actress.

'I thought you were avoiding me, actually,' Nina admitted. She had hardly spoken to her friends in the week she had been back from Tokyo. Her week off from swimming coincided with the school holidays and she thought she would get to see a lot of them. Especially Nicholas. But the world records had changed all that. It had been a week of interviews and photo shoots, meetings and contracts. It had been exciting and a bit overwhelming. But she couldn't help feel a little bit cheated. That she could think like that made her feel even worse. She should feel lucky. And appreciative.

'I told Nick you would think that, didn't I, Nick?'

'So we thought we'd get you a present just in case you were angry with us.' Nicholas presented Nina with an envelope tied with a gold ribbon. Alice giggled as she rubbed her hands together.

Nina could hardly look at Nicholas when he presented her with the envelope, even though she knew it would not be anything too personal. After all, Alice was in on the surprise too. It was the most curious gift she'd received all week. She pulled out a Sydney Symphony Orchestra pocket folder and in it was a ticket to 'An Evening with Mozart'.

Nina tried to look excited. 'Wow!'

'We thought that since we can now rattle off world record splits and personal best times like that,' Alice snapped her fingers, 'we would return the favour. Your music education needs a bit of attention and who better than us to give it to you.'

'When are we going?' She looked at Nicholas. He looked as unsure as Nina felt.

'Next Friday night.'

'What's happening on Friday?' Jake moved over to join them.

'Torture for Nina,' Alice giggled.

Jake looked over Nina's shoulder at the ticket she was holding. He couldn't talk for a few minutes for laughing.

'Torture isn't the word.'

'It'll be interesting, Jake,' Nina protested.

'In only the way a dead guy's music can be.' When nobody said anything, he continued. 'Sorry, I just prefer music that means something now.'

'You must be Jake,' Nicholas said. 'Nina has told us all about you.'

Jake and Nicholas shook hands. Again there was silence.

'What time are you going to get to the pool tomorrow?' Nina looked for neutral ground. 'There's a barbecue and open day to meet Chip Hooper,' she explained to the others. 'He's an American coach they've employed to replace Jack.'

'Actually, Nina, I'm not going tomorrow,' Jake finally answered. He looked at the floor as she spoke.

'Oh, waiting for Monday,' said Nina. 'I hate the idea of going back to the pool before the week is over. Don't really feel like I've had a break at all,' she laughed.

'Yeah, sort of.'

'What do you mean, sort of?'

Jake took a deep breath. 'I won't be there tomorrow because I'm going to Melbourne to see Jack.' He spoke so quickly Nina could hardly keep up with what he was saying.

'What do you mean?' She was repeating herself but she didn't quite understand.

'He said come and check it out so . . .' his voice trailed off. 'You know, it's not like Mum and I have any reason to stay here.'

*

'Oh no!'

Nina's whole body reverberated with a groan. She wanted

102

to die. She wanted to make it disappear. Fly around the city with a magic wand and turn them all into a puff of smoke. How many could there be? What was the circulation of a newspaper? How many people would now yell out to her in the street, just as little Christopher Kent had when she arrived at the pool that morning, 'Hey, Ninja Nina!'

She had flown into the foyer the moment it was explained to her where the little boy had seen the dreaded nickname. The broadsheet newspaper lay open in its full glory. The headline read, 'Money Talks for Ninja Nina', big, bold and black, impossible for anyone to miss. The article went on to speculate about the amounts of money Nina, and athletes like her, earned. It suggested that, with so many people living below the poverty line, the money spent on sports was now out of hand. Nina couldn't believe what she was reading.

What else could possibly go wrong? Only a week ago she thought she was invincible. She threw herself face down on the wide green bench that served as a shop counter when the pool was operational. It was closed today for the barbecue to welcome Chip Hooper.

It was her father's fault. He had been so effusive in Tokyo. Talking madly to anyone who would listen—including, it now seemed, newspaper reporters. Telling them everything about, anything she had ever done. And telling them his pet name for her.

'Ugh!' She lifted her arms, formed fists with both hands and pounded them against the counter. 'How could he have done this to me?'

'Surely things can't be that bad?'

She heard the pronunciation of 'can't' first. 'Kay-nt' rather than 'Cah-nt'. It could only be one person. She made a quick assessment of the position the speaker had found her in. Not the way to make a good impression, she decided. Did she care? Since the man was coming to coach a world record holder, a person one would expect to exhibit some dignity, she did care.

She pushed herself up off the counter and stood up straight. She wiped her face with her hands. Not really adequate, she was certain, but the best she could do. She swung herself around to face the voice.

'Depends what you call "bad"!' she laughed. She hoped it sounded like the laugh of a light-hearted, carefree kind of girl.

'Try me,' he said as he walked toward her. Chip Hooper was a very tall, thickly built man, with strawberry blonde colouring and a toothy grin.

'Well,' she looked out through the glass front of the pool to where the others were gathered, wishing she had not been so hasty to look for the newspaper. 'Your coach decides to leave. Your parents, who never really argue, start doing exactly that because they can't agree on what is right for you. Your best friend and training partner also thinks about leaving you. And to top it all off, you are humiliated in the newspapers when they use a stupid, childish nickname that they should never have known about in the first place!'

She used her hand to indicate the offending article but what was meant to be a small gesture caused the newspaper to fly off the counter. 'Drama queen,' she heard the voice in her head say. 'Behave like a child and that is how you will be treated.' She watched the newspaper float, ever so slowly, to the floor.

Chip Hooper nodded as he lifted himself up on top of the counter, sitting where the newspaper had been. He said nothing, just kept nodding. Eventually, Nina lifted herself up and sat on the counter next to him.

'I can see that would be pretty overwhelming,' he answered. His voice was deep. She noticed how he leant on the word 'over', like a low growl. But she felt relieved to hear him agree. Even though her head had been spinning with all of these things, they sounded pretty silly when said out loud. 'To any normal person, that is,' he added.

Nina looked at him.

'You are Nina Hallet, aren't you?'

She nodded. He nodded too. It was a moment before he spoke again.

'And you are the greatest backstroker in the world, are you not?'

She had not had it put in so many words. But, she supposed, yes, that was also who she was. She nodded. He nodded. Again he took a moment to speak.

'Then my guess is you are anything but normal, Nina Hallet.' He smiled at her. 'Right?'

She nodded again. This time he did not nod. Just watched her take it all in.

'It's been a big week for you, Nina. But everything is gonna work itself out,' his words were soothing. 'I'm Chip.' He held out his hand for her to shake.

She laughed at the way he introduced himself after the conversation they had just had. 'I would hope so,' she said. 'I don't usually go around saying "I am the greatest" to just anyone.'

'Well you are, so get used to it.' He punched her gently in the arm. 'You don't think I would have come all this way to coach anyone less?'

CHAPTER ELEVEN

NINA HAD SUSPECTED it would be a big night at the Opera House but she had no idea how big until the three of them reached the top of the staircase and found themselves surrounded by a sea of black ties and taffeta.

Nicholas, in the middle of the two girls, looked around the room before speaking. 'He didn't tell me it was opening night.'

'Who?' Nina asked.

'Whom,' Nicholas corrected her.

'No wonder you missed me when I was away,' she countered.

'Do you reckon they'll let me have one of those glasses of champagne?'

Alice plunged into the crowd without waiting for an answer. Nicholas and Nina followed, although there was no way they would lose her. Alice had found a way of taking the boho look in fashion to new levels. Tonight she was beaded and braided from top to toe in an orange pea coat and flowing pants that she had picked up on her 'travels' as she called them.

Alice had an endless supply of cousins in every corner of the city whom she and her family were always visiting. Through her visits Alice had gained an intimate knowledge of every weekend market bazaar around. And of every marketeer selling antique clothes. And of course they all knew her.

'That's what a girl my size has to do, Nina,' she would say. 'You can walk in and put anything on but not me. I've gotta be friends with them so when they see something my size they think "Alice" and put it away. And,' she added, 'there's stiff competition. Your *sAssy* wouldn't agree but I'm not Robinson Crusoe out there in size fourteen land.'

Nina watched Alice lean in and speak to a waiter with a drinks tray before taking a champagne flute of her own. She turned to her friends as they caught up to her.

'Champagne anyone?' She gestured with her own glass to the man and his tray.

'Just watch out for the photographers, Alice,' Nicholas warned as he took an orange juice, 'or the headline'll be "Ninja Nina's Drunken Night on the Town".' He waved his hand in front of their eyes as if to indicate the size of the headline.

Alice's mouth fell open. 'I never thought of it like that.' She looked at the champagne glass before crossing her arms in front of her body, the hand with the glass now under her orange coat. 'Do you think anyone saw me?'

'Alice, he's not serious,' Nina reassured her as she took a sip from her mineral water.

'I am serious. You saw the story the other day, Alice. The happy-go-lucky teenager who turns into a killer warrior in the water! Just give them the chance to ask if the killer is cracking up because she can't handle it and it'll be all over the papers.'

'I'm not cracking up!'

'God, Nina! I'm sorry.'

'I didn't say you were cracking up.'

'There's nothing to be sorry about, Alice.' Nina looked at Nicholas. 'What did you say then?'

'I just said we had to think about what we do or something innocent could look bad for you.'

'He's right, Nina.'

'He's not right!'

She realised she had spoken too loudly. She took a deep breath to explain but they were both looking past her with their mouths open. Nina turned around only to find herself face to face with the Prime Minister and his wife.

'Excuse me for interrupting, but my wife spotted you in the crowd and we thought we might come over and say congratulations.' The Prime Minister held out his hand to shake hers.

Nina put her own hand out automatically but all she could wonder was if he had heard her yelling at her friends. 'Thank you.'

'Are you a fan of Mozart, Nina?' the Prime Minister's wife asked as she too shook her hand.

'Ah, not really, but my friends claim they know more about swimming than they should so the least I can do is learn a bit about Mozart. This is Nicholas Coulter and Alice Hinkel,' she said, introducing her friends. What next? she thought.

The Prime Minister and his wife shook hands with Nicholas and Alice. 'Well, enjoy the concert,' the Prime Minister added before they moved off to find their seats in the Concert Hall.

They watched them walk off before anyone spoke.

'See,' said Nicholas, 'you never know who is around.'

Alice was looking at the hand the Prime Minister had just shaken. 'He is right, Nina.'

'If that's the case then I had better stop hanging out with you guys.' She turned and made her way through the crowd.

'Nina,' Nicholas ran after her.

Alice had gone around the outside of the crowd and blocked Nina's path.

'Where are you going?'

Nina stopped and Nicholas caught up.

'You can't go, Nina.' He grabbed her arm. But she shrugged him off.

'What's the point of staying?'

'What do you mean?' they asked at the same time.

'What's the point if you have to look over your shoulder all the time. If that's what it's going to be like then I don't want to go out with you guys. I'll spoil everyone's fun.'

'We're just being careful, Nina.'

'I don't want to be careful. I don't want you to worry about being careful. I just want us to be like we were before.'

'She's right, Nick.'

'Is that all you can say, Alice?'

'What are you having a go at her for, Nicholas? What's wrong with you tonight?'

Nicholas looked at his feet and then at the crowd as it made its way into the Concert Hall. The bells were ringing to indicate there were only few minutes before the concert began.

'Why are we even here?' Nina asked. 'I don't know much about this stuff but a night like this is an invitation only kind of thing.'

'You're right. We shouldn't be here.' He dug into his pocket for the tickets. 'You can go in if you want. I'm outta here.'

Nicholas tried to shove the tickets into Alice's hand but she wouldn't accept them.

'Take the tickets, Alice.' He held them in front her but she still wouldn't take them. The bells seemed to be ringing faster and faster, telling them they didn't have much time.

Alice looked at the tickets. She looked at Nina. And then at Nicholas. Tears began rolling down her cheeks.

'I was really looking forward to this night. But I'm not that desperate.' She wiped away her tears and pulled a tissue from her tiny bag. 'I don't know what your problem is, Nick. If my father had got me tickets to something like this I would just . . .'

She was having trouble keeping herself together.

Nina wasn't sure she had heard Alice right.

'Did your dad . . .?'

Nicholas dropped the hand still holding the tickets to his side. He nodded.

Just the three of them were left in the foyer. Alice finished blowing her nose. Each looked at the other. Nicholas knew he had to do something. He felt bad for upsetting Alice. She didn't deserve it.

'If you feel like giving me another chance, Alice, perhaps you'd like to come and listen to a bit of the old Wolfgang.'

Her eyes welled up with tears again. She nodded. 'Thousands wouldn't, you know.'

Nicholas lifted his arms in mock surrender. 'I know, I'm just lucky I guess.'

He turned to Nina with his best smile. 'And if I promise never to worry about being careful, ever again, would you think about joining us?'

Nina had forgotten about that argument. She wanted to ask so many other questions. But now was not the time. And there was something about that smile and the transformation it performed on his face that made her give in. Pathetic, really, she thought. There were hours ahead of her now, sitting still in the Concert Hall. Torture, as Jake had predicted, but for other reasons. How long did concerts like this go for anyway?

'Nina?'

'Yes, Alice, sorry.' She shrugged off her thoughts. 'Okay! Lead on!' she said with more enthusiasm than she felt.

*

NINJA NINA SOAKS UP SOME CULTURE

Seems its not enough these days to be a world-beating athlete! *Inside Sydney* understands that our latest world record holder, swimmer Nina Hallet, was spotted at the opening of the SSO's 'An Evening with Mozart' at the Opera House on Friday night.

Why you may ask, given we know the ninja girl's taste for the trendier hip-hop beats?

Inside Sydney can report she was overheard telling the PM, who was also in the opening night crowd, that some of her friends have had enough swimming talk and have told her to get a bit 'highbrow' or she might not have their support poolside!

Inside Sydney hears Hallet could have the last laugh. Looking sleek and cool in yet another Scarlet Rhys design (the word is she will be the face of the company in the new year) she showed her so-called highbrow friends just how to dress. Pass the word on, Nina. Whatever that orange number was, it wasn't fashion!

OLYMPIC GOLD FOR SALE
by Ron Samuels

The World Olympic Federation (WOF) has gone into damage control today following the allegations made by former East German government official, Ernst Ergsticht, to the inaugural World Summit on Drugs in Sport.

Ergsticht, who headed the Ministry for Sport and Cultural Affairs from 1979 to 1983, alleges that key members of the WOF, including the three Vice Presidents of the organisation, accepted regular cash inducements to turn a blind eye to the systematic doping of athletes both inside and outside the Iron Curtain. And that the policy continues to this day.

Ergsticht went even further, charging the West with hypocrisy in condemning the former Eastern Bloc doping programs. Ergsticht claims there was an open exchange of information between Eastern Bloc sports scientists and their free-world counterparts, particularly in the US. He believes that athletes from around the world 'benefited' from this information exchange. He said that sports medicine programs of today, while far more sophisticated, owe their success to those experiments begun in the seventies.

Ergsticht told the committee that it would be naive to believe that sport will ever be free of drugs.

The WOF's policy has always been to condemn the use of drugs in sport.

Should these corruption allegations—while not the first but certainly the most serious—be substantiated, the credibility of the organisation would be destroyed. The Olympic Games, due to open in Cape Town in less than a year's time, would surely be in doubt.

111

CHAPTER TWELVE

'NO WONDER I couldn't find that bandana,' Nina called out to her mother.

'Well, it looks better on me so I thought I'd better wear it.' Her mother smiled as she closed the newspaper.

'No, don't move. You look so comfortable!'

Nina had come out of the pool after a morning workout at the Institute of Sport to find her mum sitting on the hood of the family car, cross-legged, reading the morning paper in the sun.

'I thought you'd be hungry. We could go and get some breakfast while it's still peak hour . . .'

'In Canberra!' Nina interrupted.

Her mother laughed before going on. '. . . and then head home.'

They had come to Canberra to film a series of new commercials for the official sponsors of the Australian swim team. But it was also a good opportunity to stay a couple of days and consider the Institute as a place to prepare for the Olympics after the departure of Jack.

It wasn't that Nina didn't like Chip. But his coaching methods were different to Jack's. Nina worried that he wasn't as tough as Jack—that he didn't expect as much of her. If she was going to win gold medals at the Olympics then she couldn't afford to be slack. But Chip had only been coaching them for six weeks. Jake—who had decided to stay with the Aquanauts—suggested to Nina that maybe she was the one being tough on Chip.

Anyway, after a couple of days in Canberra she realised Jake was right. They'd had a great time—Nina and her mum—just being girls together. The late spring weather had allowed them to sit by the lake after a visit to the War Memorial or one of the other tourist sights, and just talk. Not just about swimming and the Olympics, but about all sorts of things—something they didn't seem to have much time to do at home. Another summer was almost upon them and Nina, once again, would be on and off planes, travelling to swim meets both local and overseas. And the new year would bring the Olympic year. She knew she needed to be around her family and friends more than she needed to be in Canberra with nothing more than state-of-the-art sports technology.

'There is more in the paper about the WOF covering up positive drug tests,' her mother said as she slid off the front of the car and handed Nina the paper. 'The WOF has its own self-regulating body within the organisation that investigates corruption allegations. Apparently The Standards Committee, as it is called, is also involved. You should read about it.'

'Do I have to?'

'Sam has already called,' her mother told her as they got in the car. 'He thinks it'd be better if you made a statement rather than talking to everyone. Otherwise you'll be doing interviews all day. But it's up to you.'

'What do you think?'

'A statement is probably a good idea.'

Nina looked at her mum as she buckled her seat belt. Ever since the night Nina had overheard her mother and father talking about postponing school, her mother had been making some very un-Annette-like statements. The school issue had been resolved with the decision to hire a tutor when Nina went into Year 11. Nina would go to school when she could, and the tutor would work with her teachers to keep her up to date with anything she missed.

But agreeing to the release of a prepared statement rather than appearing in the press with an intelligent opinion wasn't something her mum would normally go along with.

'But now that I'm just in it for the money it might look like I'd do anything for a gold medal.'

The seat belt sprang out of its buckle. Her mother leant back against the door as if to get Nina into better focus. 'I want you to stop that right now, okay. You are not to start judging yourself on the basis of a couple of opinion pieces in a newspaper romanticising the good old days of Australian sport. These people have no concept of what it's like to be a swimmer these days,' she said as she started the car. 'You'd think they'd be happy for you,' she added, almost to herself.

'I was just joking, Mum.'

'But has anyone else said that to you?'

Nina shrugged. 'No.'

Her mother relaxed. 'No, no one would because it's a stupid thing to think. There isn't a person in the world that would think you should knock back all these great offers. You've worked bloody hard. It's pure jealousy, Nina. Do you want to go to that cafe we went to yesterday?'

Nina nodded. 'But why do you want me to hide now?'

'Who said anything about hiding? Sam said a statement would save you a lot of hassle. It has nothing to do with hiding. You can still state your opinion.'

'Sounds stage-managed and bland.' Nina was teasing her mum by repeating the words she so often used to describe athletes and the media.

Her mother glared at her as she rammed the seat belt back into its buckle. 'It's about being practical, Nina. You said you've got exams to study for when you get home. You promised to do the on-line chat for *Sports Mad!* readers. And you have two lunches to speak at next week. But if you think you have time, then by all means spend the day doing interviews.'

Nina knew she had chosen the wrong issue to use as an example. It would be much easier to release a statement. Even she had to admit that. But Nina would rather have a disagreement with her mum than find her retreating from her own ideas because of the pressure Nina's swimming might place on her.

'Did anyone else call?' Nina decided to drop the subject for now.

'Before eight in the morning?' Her mother took a quick look at Nina. 'Who were you expecting?'

'I dunno.'

'Don't know. Two words.'

Nina didn't repeat the offending words. But it made her smile—evidence of the old spunky Annette. Maybe she was overreacting.

'I can taste those blueberry pancakes already,' Nina's mother said, as they neared the Belconnen cafe they had discovered yesterday. 'I know I shouldn't but I've got to have them again!'

The subject of food reminded Nina of the television crew that had been at the pool that morning.

In light of the latest drug scandal, a weekly science program was doing a story on the developments in sports science. They were comparing some of the antiquated experiments 'experts' used to perform on athletes with the modern, high-tech equipment at the Institute.

For the cameras, a couple of the swimmers, including Nina, got into a strange contraption that once tested strength-to-weight ratios. After being locked into the thing they were lowered under the water and then had to breathe out and push off the bottom of the pool with as much force as they could, all at the same time. The swimmers could hardly do what was required of them because they all got a fit of the giggles every time they tried.

For Nina, the test showed she would have to weigh five kilos less than she did to be capable of swimming the world record times she set in Tokyo two months before. The results were similarly ludicrous for all the swimmers.

Brian Cook, who Nina knew as the Australian head coach, was also the coach at the Institute. 'You'd wouldn't have any strength at that weight,' he told Nina.

But walking through the change rooms after the workout she caught sight of her reflection in the mirror. She knew that the test she had just done had no basis in fact. But Nina could see that her body was definitely changing. She was certainly not the shapeless little girl she had been a year ago. She had gained a few curves, mostly through her hips and legs. She was taller, so not everything was unwelcome. But what if puberty came on with a vengeance and changed her body completely in the next year? There were horror stories about stuff like that. Girls never getting near the times that they had swum in previous years. Fat piling on in an unstoppable fashion. She'd never had to think about the food she ate but maybe it was time. She resolved to be careful with everything she put in her mouth. Maybe she shouldn't eat pancakes this morning.

Nina's mum interpreted her silence as something else. 'How is Nicholas?' she asked as innocently as possible.

'Good, I think. Why?'

'That's who you were expecting to call, wasn't it?'

'Before eight in the morning?'

Her mother didn't laugh. She shot Nina a sideways glance. 'You like him, don't you.' It was a statement not a question.

'Mu-um.'

Her mother chuckled.

Her mother knew too much. Nina *had* hoped Nicholas would call. They had played a kind of phone-tag for a few days now. If only she and Nicholas had been able to spend a couple of days together sitting and talking in the spring sunshine. In the last term everyone had been flat out cramming for Year 10 final exams and Nina was no exception. It was just one more thing she had to do. Long idle chats on the telephone were a distant memory. There had been no chance to ask him about the concert tickets. Or about his father. Whenever they were together Alice was always with them. Even at the concert she had sat between them. There was no reason for it not to be so. But that kiss at the eisteddfod seemed a long time ago. 'You wouldn't even call it a kiss,' a voice said. Nina chose not to respond.

'Here we are,' her mother declared as she pulled into a car spot.

'Good,' said Nina. What a morning! She reminded herself to play music on the drive home from Canberra. Anything to distract her.

'Have you got your beanie, Nina? It's too cold for you to be walking around with a wet head.'

'Yes, Mum.' Her mother waited until she had retrieved the hat from between the car seats where it had fallen. The car locking system bleeped into action. She followed her mother into the cafe. Maybe the pancakes would stop her thinking.

WE'RE NOT CHEATS

by Ron Samuels

The sports world is in turmoil following the startling allegations by former East German minister, Ernst Ergsticht, at the World Summit on Drugs in Sport. His claims include the collusion of Eastern Bloc and US scientists and sports officials, not just in assisting the use of performance-enhancing drugs by their athletes, but in bribing senior WOF officials to turn a blind eye to the positive drug tests made by Olympic medal winners over the past thirty years.

It is understood that at least two former US sports scientists and a former WOF

Standards Committee member have backed up the allegations, although they are unwilling to be named.

In the US, past and present Olympic medallists have presented a petition to the US Congress denying the allegations and calling for further proof.

At home, Australian athletes have called for the US Congress to investigate the allegations and, if substantiated, have demanded that the WOF officials, including President Philippe Aresto, be removed from office.

Dual world record holder, Nina Hallet, in a statement issued through her management, backed up the call for further proof.

'I wish to believe in the ideals of the Olympic movement and that those ideals are upheld by people in the most senior positions of the WOF as well as athletes, like me, who aspire to be part of the Olympic family. We need to be reassured that those who bring home medals from next year's Cape Town Olympic Games have won them fairly and in the true spirit of competition.'

HALLET STRUGGLES TO FIND FORM
by Ron Samuels

Even a return to the site of her first international success wasn't enough to help Nina Hallet find her world record-breaking form at the World Short Course titles here at the Manchester Aquatic Centre today.

'I'm trying not to worry about it,' she told reporters after she won the 200m Backstroke title easily, but in a time two seconds outside her personal best.

'I guess there are all sorts of reasons. We're in hard training. We've been on tour for a few weeks. You know, you can't expect miracles,' she laughed. 'It's just a bit different to last year when every time I got in the water I seemed to swim a best time. But, you know, it's January and the Olympics aren't till July so I've got a long way to go.'

In the last six weeks Hallet has become the unofficial spokesperson for Australian athletes as the US Congress investigates the WOF bribery allegations. But when asked if the controversy could be affecting her swimming, she shrugged it off.

'It has tended to dominate conversation lately,' she said in a classic under-statement. 'But it has to be dealt with if we are truly serious about getting rid of drugs in sport. And this is the time. But I'm not going to let it affect my swimming.'

CHAPTER THIRTEEN

NINA LEANT AGAINST the brick wall outside the music room. She could hear her friend working diligently at the piano on a piece she didn't recognise.

It had been a long time since she'd hesitated before entering a room and interrupting him. Not that she didn't respect his practice time. But as they had become friends she was pretty confident that her interjections brought him an entertaining break from something that was often causing him intense frustration.

That confidence had gone for the moment. She had hardly seen her friends in the past few months. Snatched hours here and there. E-mails to and from wherever she was overseas. And now everyone was back in Year 11 and already talking about the HSC. Nina had missed the Year 10 formal because of an altitude training camp in Albuquerque. That meant the last time they had really got dressed up and gone out together was that night at the Opera House, almost five months ago. And she couldn't even say that had been a success. Nicholas's warnings from that night had come true, although Alice had brushed off the pointed attack of her in the paper.

'Wouldn't be caught dead in what they call fashion, Nina,' she had told her.

But Alice hadn't appeared at any of Nina's public appearances since. Nina missed her but she would never again ask Alice to put herself in a position where she could be made a fool of.

Even worse, Shan was doing work experience at *Femme* the week Nina was part of a photo shoot for the magazine. The readers had chosen Nina as the celebrity they would most like to have as their best friend. Shan had told everyone at the magazine that she and Nina were real-life best friends. So Shan had been sent on the photo shoot.

Shan had hovered close to Nina during the entire day, even interjecting during the interview to add her own thoughts! At the end of the day the journalist had insisted on a photo of the two 'best friends'. Nina couldn't say no. It would have only made her look like a complete bitch, she'd thought. Better to grin and bear it.

Without Nina's knowledge the magazine had then sent the photo to *Inside Sydney* to promote the upcoming magazine spread. It had appeared in last week's Sunday paper and Nina hadn't had a chance to explain the situation to Alice or Nicholas.

Nina pushed herself off the wall. If she didn't walk into the music room soon the lunch break would be over and she would miss the opportunity to talk to Nicholas. Just go in as though everything is normal, she told herself.

He looked up as she reached the piano.

'Oh my God!' he cried. 'I remember you. What was your name again? Nelly, Nell, Nan, no, I think it's Nina. That's right, isn't it? Nina?'

She rolled her eyes. 'All right, all right.'

He didn't seem to be bothered by the interruption. And she was certainly happy to see him and to have him to herself. She crossed her legs and sat on the floor next to the piano chair.

'How's it going?'

'Okay, I guess.' He shrugged his shoulders and ran his hand lightly along the keys. 'First time I've tried to play it.'

'I didn't think I had heard it before.'

He smiled at her. 'Is that right?'

'Well, I've heard most of what you play,' she protested.

He laughed, looked back at the keys, then lifted his hand and softly played a few notes. The soundtrack to the scene they were acting out, Nina thought.

'Haven't I, Nicholas?'

'More than most, I'd say.'

She watched him as his hands moved over the keys. She wanted to just blurt out the questions she had been waiting months to ask. Why did your father get us tickets to the symphony if he hated music? Why did your mother think he loved music more than her?

But she hadn't been alone with him like this for so long. And the music he was playing for them was so soothing. She didn't want to ruin it by making him angry.

Nina got up, unable to sit still any longer. She walked over to the window. A game of touch football was being played on the field; a mixed game of basketball on the courts a little further in the distance. Nicholas continued to play.

'Don't suppose you've ever played basketball, Nicholas?'

It was such an odd question for her to ask that it brought his piano playing to a halt.

'Not recently, Nina, no.'

'Me, neither. Looks like fun though.'

'S'pose so.' He couldn't tell what was going on in her mind. 'We've got a hoop set up in the back yard, though.'

'You have?' That brought her attention back to the room.

'I think so.'

'But, you don't know?'

He shrugged.

'We used to have one but it drove my mother mad. You know, the ball doing all that banging against the wall and stuff when my brother and his friends came over.'

'Getting rebounds, you mean.'

121

'At least I know it isn't there anymore.'

He started playing again. It took him a moment to speak. 'My mother always tried to get us to play hoops with her.'

Nina couldn't believe what she was hearing. 'You and your dad?'

He nodded. 'I could never really see the point.'

She smiled. Such a Nicholas thing to say. She imagined his mother saying—as her own mother did sometimes—'don't know where I got you from!'

'Your mother liked sport, though,' she said, hoping she didn't sound like she was pushing for information. Again she waited a few agonising moments for him to speak.

'Mad for it,' he seemed to smile at the thought. 'Bit like you.'

Nina blushed. She tried one more question. 'And your dad?'

'He got really bad arthritis in his hands when he was quite young.' Nicholas finally looked up at her. 'From playing the piano, of all things. So, you know, it ruined his basketball career!'

She laughed with him but she understood that she'd been given as much information as she would get today. A piano player whose hands were injured. She had met so many athletes in her time that never let go of wondering what they might have achieved if only they hadn't been injured.

'But if we still have that hoop up you may come over and use it,' he offered.

'Not in the near future.'

He couldn't work her out. 'Why not?'

'You know, might twist my ankle or something. Bit more at stake, these days. Just until the Olympics, that is.'

'Oh! How are you with it all?'

'Oh, fine,' she said.

She looked at him to see if he would buy it like everyone

else did. He raised his eyebrows. She knew she could be honest with Nicholas. But where would she begin?

'Just hope it's all worth it, you know.'

He nodded. He could only imagine what she was going through. 'Well,' he said, 'I've always thought basketball a highly overrated game.'

They both laughed.

'You'd better come over here then,'

She shook her head, not understanding. 'Come on!' He moved to one side of the piano stool and patted the spot next to him.

Nina walked over and sat down. Just sitting beside him made her feel better.

'Come on, hands up like this.' Nina imitated the position of his hands. 'That's good but don't get all limp-wristed on me.' He fixed her wrist position. 'That's it. Now, hit those keys there, that's the chord of C.'

Nina did as she was told and a half note seeped from the instrument.

'Well, there is room for improvement but at least it's an injury-free pastime.' He gave her a nudge with his shoulder. 'And don't think this is some charity class either. I've been reading about you and I know what you're worth. Don't think I won't charge accordingly.'

CHAPTER FOURTEEN

NINJA-NINA DEFENDS DRUG CHEATS
by Rick Jeffries

As hope mounts around the world that performance-enhancing drugs might finally be eliminated from the world of sport, drug cheats have found a surprising ally in dual world record holder, Nina Hallet.

Speaking on Channel 4's public affairs program, *Behind the Headlines*, Hallet said it's a more complicated issue than just saying yes or no.

'What if you are a really good runner?' she asked host Michael Warne. 'From what everyone says, most of the track and field athletes take drugs. What do you do? Where's the level playing field?

'And what if you are a runner from a family that doesn't have a lot of money? Not winning a gold medal is one thing. But now not winning means you don't have the chance of earning any money—or being rich and famous and admired. You can change your life with your running. All you have to do is take drugs. And everyone else is doing it so what's the difference? I just hope that people who are going around blaming athletes for taking drugs are the kind of people who know that, if they were in a similar situation, then they would be able to say no.'

The World Olympic Federation's newly formed Drug Task Force is heading the internal investigation into the bribery allegations levelled at some of its members three months ago. It is due to release its report within weeks.

'I didn't say that.'

Nina threw the paper down on the dining room table. She looked at each of them. It was becoming commonplace now. Impromptu meetings to go over the appropriate thing for Nina to say at a public appearance. Or, worse, revising the way she could have said something after it had appeared on television or in the newspaper.

She reached over and grabbed one of the chocolate biscuits off the plate on the table. Her parents and Sam had obviously been waiting for her for a while. Coffee and biscuits had gone around more than once.

'You never used to eat chocolate biscuits.' It was her father who spoke.

'Well, I do now.'

She took the bite first and looked at him second. She regretted it instantly. She shocked herself with her own petulance sometimes.

Anyway, how could she tell him she would deal with it in a few moments when she went to her room? Disgust rippled through her. She shook it out. Walked a few paces across the room into the kitchen and leant against the fridge. She couldn't rest there. Moved to the bench and lifted herself up onto the counter.

A month before she had been on a training camp with the national team in Albuquerque in New Mexico. The Australian team went there regularly to train at altitude, which was thought to improve racing performance. Nina had always loved the camps. The training was hard but there was something about the thin air that made her feel giddy and not quite herself.

But this last camp had been much more difficult. She knew it was her second last chance to train at altitude before the Olympics. She had to make the most of it. She trained as hard as she could. But no matter how hard she pushed herself in the water she could never exhaust herself enough to stop that gnawing, anxious sensation. She didn't know where it came from, although it was obvious everyone was pretty tense. Albuquerque was supposed to give all swimmers the chance to have a few weeks break from 'Olympic-gate' as Dominic called it. But it was all anyone talked about.

Inevitably the conversation would come back to what to say to the press. One of these discussion sessions deteriorated into an attack on the swimmers who were getting all the press.

'We would all look much better if those of us who have been around for a while handled the PR,' Jebby Cross stood as she spoke, just to make her point.

Ursula Best, sitting behind Nina, said, 'That's right,' just loudly enough for Nina to hear.

Nina tried to tell herself that they were just trying to help. But there was a lot of talk in dormitory rooms and change rooms that Nina wasn't asked to take part in. In fact conversation often stopped if she walked up and joined a group. She told herself she was imagining it. But that didn't really work.

Not that it mattered, she told herself. She had her friends. But even when she was sitting down laughing with Dominic and some of the boys at post-training breakfast, the gnawing feeling would find her. She did everything she could to banish it. Concentrated really hard on what was being said. Laughed, even when there was nothing to really laugh at. Talked, even when there was really nothing to say. But the harder she tried the louder the feeling got. It was like the vibrating interference on the radio before the mobile phone went off. And the vibration would work through her entire her body.

Eventually, when other distractions didn't work, she would reach for a piece of leftover toast on the breakfast table. And then another. And then something else. Until her tummy was full and the vibrations would stop.

But then her head would start. Anger. Frustration. 'Stupid girl,' said the voice. 'Ruining your chances of everything. Letting everyone down.' The promise not to do it again.

And then she overheard a conversation in the toilets on the

attributes of a well-timed laxative. She admonished herself for even considering it. But when an extra two kilos added themselves to her body she found herself in an Albuquerque drug store. It was hard to find what she was looking for while constantly looking over her shoulder to make sure no one was following.

After about fifteen minutes of prowling around the aisles and telling the shop assistant she didn't need her help, she finally admitted defeat. She even had to repeat her request because she spoke too quietly the first time. Nina couldn't remember ever feeling more mortified.

The pill had the desired effect, physically. The weight gain was halted. But Nina had not anticipated the mental effect. Disgust seeped its way deeper into her limbs. It turned to loathing. She found less and less to like about herself. She resolved to stop the cycle. But everywhere she went food seemed to scream out to her. Particularly when she was worried about saying the wrong thing. Which was pretty constant these days.

'It's not that bad, is it?'

Nicholas's voice broke her thoughts. For a moment she thought she had spoken out loud. Confessed. But when she looked up she found him with the newspaper in his hand. He'd just read the article that had brought them all together.

'It's not that Nina has said anything bad, Nicholas,' said her mother, 'it's just the way it is interpreted in a headline: "Ninja-Nina Defends Drug Cheats".'

Nicholas had only heard about these sessions. It was by chance he was now witnessing one. He had caught the bus home with Nina. They had been at the beach, with a few of the others, enjoying the last of days of summer.

'I don't even know why we are having this conversation,' Nina said. 'You know what I said. You were there. You didn't think I'd said anything wrong then.'

She waited for one of them to speak. She appealed to Nicholas. 'It was a live interview and the paper has just lifted the most sensational stuff. I did say the WOF should be sacked if it is guilty. But I don't know what would happen then. I don't know if you could even have an Olympic games. What would we do then?' Nina didn't like the sense of relief that thought brought.

'Otherwise, I was just saying that whenever anything is written about me it is usually accompanied by speculation about how much I am worth. The other day I read a newspaper article about how much money each country gives their athletes for gold medals. Even poor countries offer apartments and cars. People cheat on their tax for a lot less, you know,' she tried to make him understand.

She looked out the window and thought about the interview. She had thought she was presenting a unique argument. She didn't realise how it would be interpreted.

'And what about that guy on the way home today?' she said to Nicholas. 'Lecturing me about what a disgrace we all were. "Not like Dawn Fraser and Murray Rose who swam for the glory of their country!"' She repeated his words, wagging her finger as the man on the bus had. 'Shoot me for swimming in the wrong century.'

She looked at all of them. At her mother. 'Do you think I said the wrong thing, Mum?'

For a moment there was silence. Her mother looked at her father and then Sam.

'No, love, I don't.'

'Oh, Annette.'

'What, Dad?'

'Nothing, Nina.'

'It must be something,' she countered.

'Sam is just trying to help you, Nina. Didn't you hear anything he said last week?'

'But that was the same thing, Dad. A headline that had nothing to do with what I was saying.' Again she turned to Nicholas.

'At a lunch last week this journalist was asking me to justify why sport got all the money that should be spent on schools and hospitals. And why sport got money when there were young Australians struggling in other fields of endeavour.' She imitated the journalist's pompous tones. 'I was sitting next to this girl who was an amazing mathematician. She'd finished high school at, you know, five or something.'

Nina got a smile from her friend. They both knew she was exaggerating.

'Anyway, she was studying at an Institute in Stockholm or somewhere but wasn't given any sort of grant or anything. I agreed with him, it was unfair. So I was like, great, give them all the money if it means the focus shifts off me for a while.' She got down off the bench.

'But as I said to him, I doubt that would happen because we all know that, even years ago, when there was no money, Australians expected their athletes to be winners. That's right isn't it, Dad?'

She wanted to put him on the spot too. After all, she had heard this argument many times at the dinner table. It was usually when her mother had gone on the rampage about politicians hiding behind sports heroes so that attention was drawn away from all the money taken from public schools and hospitals to fund sports programs. Nina's father argued that was what Australians wanted.

She waited for her father to answer her but he just glared at her.

'That headline,' she continued, 'was "Ninja Nina Says Leave Me Alone." And then, of course, there were all sorts of psychological studies about me and whether I was "coping".'

'Gee, I don't know why!' Nicholas tried to make Nina laugh.

She looked straight at him. 'What do you mean by that?'

He sighed, willing her not to get so worked up. 'It's a joke.'

'Nina,' Sam's voice sounded quiet and controlled compared to the pitch Nina had worked herself up to. 'No one said these are easy subjects but we just want to find a few easy answers for you so that you are not misrepresented.'

'You don't care if I am misrepresented, Sam,' Nina argued. 'You just care what the sponsors think.' She looked at Nicholas again but this time he looked away from her.

But it didn't stop her talking.

'It seems sponsors only read headlines. Not any further than that. And my headlines don't look that good. Do they Sam? Not that anyone could look good with that ridiculous nickname they use. But thanks to my stupid father I have to put up with that too.' She was barely holding herself together.

'Nina,' her mother pleaded.

'Well, I haven't heard anyone say *he* made a mistake.' She wished she could make herself stop talking but words were tumbling out uncontrollably. She was sure she would never see Nicholas again. She had become the shrew from the Shakespeare play they had studied last year.

'We all just want to hear you sounding positive, Nina,' Sam tried again to reason with her. 'If you're seen to be defending athletes who take drugs, people might assume *you* take drugs. We just have to be careful. These are huge issues that you are dealing with, Nina. For anyone, never mind someone who is about to turn sixteen next week and trying to win an Olympic gold medal.'

Which I have no chance of doing if I swim anything like I did last week, Nina thought. She'd gone to Auckland for a Women's International meet and she still couldn't get any-where near what she and Chip considered good times. She felt like an elephant trying to swim.

'Now you're patronising me. My age has never been an issue before.'

'Nina, I've just about had enough of this!' Her father got up from his chair.

'Me too,' she yelled back at him, 'but I don't have that luxury, do I?'

'Don't speak to your father like that, Nina,' her mother admonished her.

'But . . .'

'Nina!'

'Geoff, stop yelling,' she pleaded

'I am not yelling, Annette.'

'You are.'

'It's okay, Mum.'

'It's not okay, Nina.'

'Can't I at least say what I want to in my own house,' her father exploded at her mother.

The front door opened just as Nina's father finished his outburst. It slammed hard, handle into wall. Nina's brother stood for a moment in the doorway, surfboard tucked under one arm, a strap of his backpack slung over the other. He looked at them all. Nina had to move out of the way of his surfboard as he lunged at the table for the remaining chocolate biscuit.

'Yet another happy day in the Hallet household I see,' he said as he put the entire biscuit into his mouth. 'Good one, Nina,' he added as he walked through to his bedroom.

NINJA-NINA RETREATS

by Ron Samuels

After a disappointing summer of swimming it was announced today that Sydney swim sensation Nina Hallet has withdrawn from all further public commitments from now until the Olympic Games in July.

Manager Sam Thompson issued the statement this morning.

'Nina regrets disappointing people but hopes everyone will understand the enormous pressure she and other Australian athletes have been under for the last couple of months. While she recognises the responsibility she has to her sponsors and her fans she also has a responsibility to herself to make sure she has done everything possible to prepare for this year's Olympic Games.'

This season Hallet has failed to reproduce the form that last year culminated in world records in the 100m and 200m Backstroke at the Pan Pacific Swimming Championships in Tokyo.

Her poor performances in the pool, combined with her lack of diplomacy during the Olympic drug scandal, have dented the popularity of the young woman who was expected to take out this year's Young Australian of the Year Award. The honour instead went to outstanding young physicist Max Mahoney.

In an ironic twist the World Olympic Federation's Drug Task Force found in its report to the US Congress this week that the allegations made four months ago by East German Ernst Ergsticht are unfounded. The five WOF members who stood down while being investigated have now been reinstated to their former positions within the organisation. Ernst Ergsticht was last night unavailable for comment.

Hallet has two months to regain her edge before the Olympic Selection trials in May.

CHAPTER FIFTEEN

NINA SLID OUT of bed and tiptoed to the door of her room. No one was awake. The whispered mutterings that had come from her parents' room had long stopped. All she could hear was the heavy breathing of her father's sleep. Her brother's room was silent. Just to be sure, she pushed her bedroom door closed, praying the hinges would not give her away.

Back at her bed, she turned on the sidelight. As the light filled the room, she caught sight of the framed concert poster of the Red Hot Chili Peppers' tour of Europe, which hung above the light. The band had been staying at the same hotel as the Australian team when they were at a swim meet in Prague. On the morning the team was leaving, Nina had got up early for a walk across the Charles Bridge. Thinking she had the bridge to herself she had been startled by a voice offering to take a picture of her with her own camera. Turning, she'd found herself face to face with Flea, the Peppers' lead singer, and a couple of the road crew. They had all walked back to the same hotel, and had eaten break-fast together. Before she left the hotel that morning she had an autographed tour poster. The Chili Peppers had a new fan.

Nina moved to her desk, flicked the switch of her standard desk lamp and plonked herself down, cross-legged, in the middle of the bedroom.

All around her there were pictures, trinkets, photos, prints—all mementos collected on her travels. Some were photos she had taken herself. Above her bed were magazine proofs of the first photos published by *sAssy*, all framed. Another wall displayed a series on Barcelona, which a travel magazine had published, together with the story she had written to go with the pictures.

Above her bed hung a photo of Dominic which she had taken when they were teamed together for a story in *Sports Mad!* magazine. The photographer was a young guy who'd always answered, with great patience, Nina's endless enquiries about his profession. He'd let Nina take some shots on his camera while Dominic was having his make-up done. She had taken a goofy picture of her friend reflected in the mirror. Not original she knew, but the magazine used it in the photo spread and she was credited with the shot. It went on to win an award for the magazine.

Surrounding her was her life as she had come to know it in the last two years. Nowhere was there any evidence of the little girl that existed before that.

'What a difference,' she sighed.

Two years ago she'd been up all night, too excited to sleep after making her first Australian team. Tonight she'd just made another Australian team. But this one was a bit different. Nina had been selected for her first Olympic team. It had been her goal ever since she could remember, the thing she had always dreamt about. But tonight the only feeling keeping her awake was that of overwhelming relief.

'And determination, she whispered.

She got up and moved to the walls and began removing the paraphernalia she had been looking at. The walls were needed for far more important business now. Tears began to roll down her face.

'This is not how making an Olympic team is supposed to feel,' a voice said from somewhere inside her head.

She ignored it. What did the voice know?

134

'It's supposed to be even more exciting than that first time,' it continued.

'It is exciting,' Nina whispered, as she wiped away tears. This was no time to indulge her emotions. 'But I have a job to do now.'

From under her desk she pulled a large box. It was a disorganised jumble of cardboard, papers, brushes, paints, pens, pencils; you never really knew what you might find in there. Her father called it her junk box. From inside it she pulled out a roll of sheets of multi-coloured cardboard and proceeded to unroll them. She had been meaning to do this for a few weeks now.

Everything had seemed much easier since her decision to withdraw from the spotlight. The announcement had brought a flood of public sympathy. Where she had been too nervous to walk out her door for fear of what someone might say, now everywhere she went people seemed desperate to prove how understanding they could be.

The strange pain that she had learned to live with, right in the groove where her neck met the base of her skull, seemed to miraculously disappear. Her mum and dad seemed to smile more. No one was angry.

Nina taped a couple of the cardboard sheets together then sat back on her haunches, visualising what she wanted to create. It would be a big, bold graph—that she would stick on the wall next to her bed—with the times she had recorded for her backstroke races over the past two years. She would chart the times as they dropped all the way to the world records, then she would bravely highlight the plateau she seemed to be experiencing now. Then, most importantly, she would brightly predict the new marks she aimed to set at the Olympics in two months time.

She grabbed a soft lead pencil to begin sketching an outline of the graph. Eventually she would include other elements.

'Collage, mixed media,' she laughed quietly to herself. She felt better already. 'A work in progress,' she added.

She began thinking ahead. She saw herself scouring all the magazines in the house for every image of success she could find. She made a plan to keep her smallest camera with her at all times just in case she could add her own pictures to the art work.

Her mind wandered back over the past couple of months. She had been so sure she would be lying in bed tonight, after the final night of the Olympic trials, swamped with the satisfaction of success. She had not expected to break her world records again at the Trials. Well, maybe she hoped she would. Chip had talked about competing at the Olympic Selection trials while still in heavy training. But she knew the workouts in the week leading up to the trials had been easier. She hadn't argued with him though, hadn't complained that he was too easy on her, as she had done before.

With the easier workouts she had silently hoped she would find that magic glide that had preceded every good swim over the past couple of years. Every time she dived in to warm up at the Olympic trials, she had floated for a moment longer than necessary. Waiting, feeling, praying for something she wasn't sure she could find. She would take a few slow strokes, giving her body a little bit more time to find that elusive slipstream. But it had not appeared all weekend.

'But, that's okay,' she reassured herself as she grabbed the coloured crayons she would use for the first section of her graph.

Even without the magic feeling, she had made the team. She had won both the backstroke events although they were not impressive wins by her own standards.

'But you did win, Nina,' she told herself as she used the colour residue on her fingers to work the cardboard.

For the first time she had experienced how it felt to have

some of the crowd cheering for another girl, Rose Manning. Rose was the same age as Nina and usually came fourth or fifth in the finals. But she had swum best times at the trials and had made the Olympic team as the second backstroker. Jebby Cross had announced her retirement after missing out on the team. Nina had hardly spoken to her old rival since Albuquerque so she was surprised when Jebby had sought her out on the last night of the trials.

'All you had to do was get on the team, Nina. Don't worry about the times you swam this weekend. Eric will help you get you those medals. I told him he's got to look after you.' Eric Andersen was Jebby's long-time coach. He was also an Australian coach and trained Nina whenever she travelled with the national team.

Jebby had given Nina a hug. She had had tears in her eyes. 'The Olympics, they're like nothing else,' she'd added. 'Be tough.'

Nina continued to decorate the cardboard. How much tougher could it get? Surely she had come through the worst of it. And not just the drug scandal. She'd also managed to give up 'her little habit', as she called it. She'd not used the last packet of laxatives she'd bought. It remained, unopened, in her hiding place at the bottom of the big drawer full of sweaters, in her wardrobe. And Nina had every intention of it staying that way.

Admittedly she had replaced the habit with a strict food diary, entering everything she ate throughout the day and giving herself a score out of ten at the end of it. There were less than perfect days. Like the day her mum and dad had returned from three days in the Hunter Valley and had brought home the most amazing cheese. It was one of Nina's great weaknesses and she had eaten three crackers smothered in the stuff. It was like eating heaven, Nina had thought. But so fattening. Her willpower had faltered but even though the temptation was enormous, the packet in the drawer remained unopened. She was amazed how that small achievement had far outweighed the guilt associated with eating the cheese.

Sometimes the diary made her feel much better too. There were days she did not seem to make any progress. Her back-stroke felt clunky in the water. She was told something else Shan said. Nicholas was busy practising. Or she attended a sponsor's lunch where the enthusiasm people felt for the year and what she might achieve was so out of sync with her own.

But she would get into bed and look at her food diary and see that at least in that area of her life she had been good. Not the failure she spent all day telling herself she was.

It was all slightly compulsive, she knew that. But it was better than swallowing the little brown pills. And it wasn't as though she were the only girl with an unusual food fixation at school, or at the pool.

Besides, if she could stay off the laxatives there would never be a moment like her last purchase.

'Is this an ongoing problem, Nina?' she'd heard the shop assistant ask.

She hadn't known whether to look up from the magazine she'd buried her head in, but the woman was staring at her.

'Pardon?' She had pretended not to hear.

'You were in Elizabeth Street about ten days ago,' the woman had said. 'I run both stores.'

Nina had shaken her head. 'Not me, no,' she'd smiled her best smile. 'Must have been someone else.'

The woman had kept looking at her, then she'd just nodded and rung up the sale. Nina had gone back, casually, to her magazine. But she'd kept her head down and had got out of the store as quickly as possible.

Imagine if the woman was the kind who called up the newspapers. Nina read all the gossip columns over the next few days but nothing appeared. You never could be sure. One gossip magazine even gave an e-mail address for people to report 'if there is something you know that we don't'. Nina knew there were people so desperate to see their name in the newspaper or their face on television that they would think nothing of humiliating others to achieve that.

Nina pushed the thought from her mind. She had been lucky that time. She sat back and inspected her poster. It was definitely bright. Loud, even.

'Screams at you really,' Nina giggled to herself.

The reporters at the pool over the weekend had been really nice to her actually. Not so long ago she was sure everyone thought of her as just another teenage sports brat. Tonight everyone had been more than generous.

'Not that you were the story this time,' she reminded herself.

There was a bunch of new faces. New hopes. Including Rose Manning. Nina had been surprised at how brash the new Australian representative had been.

'I made a promise to myself that I would be number one in the world this year and I'm not stopping 'til I get there,' she had told reporters as she sat next to Nina in the after-race press conference.

Nina had looked at the girl who was so determined to beat her. Had she ever been that confident? Ever wanted to win that badly? Ever been so fearless?

Nina had looked at the reporters standing around the room to see how they interpreted such a declaration. Mostly they were just recording it in whatever media they worked. Except Ron Samuels. He had lifted his head from the page he was scribbling on, looked straight at Nina and given her wink. She had smiled at him and silently thanked him for his support.

'Upstart,' she muttered to herself as she put her crayons down and reached for the double-sided tape. She had to smile though, Rose Manning had reminded her of what the Olympic year was about. It was about being brave and standing up to the challenge.

Nina had to stretch her arms out as wide as she could to hold the poster she'd spent half the night making. She stood on her bed and shuffled across, struggling to keep her balance. There was still some collage work to be done to finish it but she couldn't wait to get it up on the wall. When she was sure the poster was fixed securely she stood back to survey the result. It was the first thing she would see when she woke up in the morning, the last thing when she went to bed at night. She had a feeling it was all going to work.

'You see, *I* am number one in the world, Rose Manning.' Nina sat down on her bed. It felt good. 'Catch me if you can, sweetheart.' It was an endearment Nicholas used more and more these days. Usually with a hint of sarcasm. Nina looked at the mess she had made of her room. It could stay there until the morning. She climbed under the doona and curled herself up into a little ball. Without even turning off the lights, she fell straight to sleep.

CHAPTER SIXTEEN

NINA THREW HER carry-all over her shoulder.

'Gotta go,' she told Tamasin.

'Should have been hours ago,' the *sAssy* editor replied as she studied contact sheets through a magnifying glass. She looked up at Nina. 'He'll kill me, you know.'

'I doubt that,' Nina replied with a grin.

'Nevertheless, don't come in tomorrow, Nina.'

Nina stopped in the doorway.

'I promised Sam guest editing would require you to do no more than meet me and Judith for lunch, throw a few ideas around and then we would go ahead and put "your" issue together.'

'But, I'm on holidays, Tam,' she reminded her. 'I'm not getting tired. I'm not rundown. Call Chip. I'm swimming better every day.'

'It's a fluke we have you, Nina,' Tamasin countered. 'Lucky you and I were at the same launch. Sam had already said no to this and you changed his mind. So let's not push it.'

'Half a day?'

'Stay home and rest. You have another training camp in two weeks and then the Games.'

'Now you sound like him,' Nina knew she was being cheeky.

'Out,' Tamasin ordered. She pointed to the door. But she kept her head down in case she was blushing.

Nina knew the *sAssy* editor was right. She and Tamasin had

met by coincidence at the launch of a new fragrance at a city hotel. Nina discovered that Sam had rejected Tamasin's requests for Nina to 'guest edit' an issue of *sAssy* until after the Olympics. But Nina had been so excited by the concept that she visited Sam's office the day after the launch with a manila folder full of ideas for 'her' issue and pleaded with him to let her do it. A conference between Sam, her parents and Chip concluded that anything that made her like the 'old Nina' was worth a try. So Nina got her way.

There were strict conditions: it had to be after the Olympic trials, in school holidays, and Nina's input was to be kept to a minimum. Nina didn't know what was more thrilling—her issue of the magazine or the gradual realisation that Sam and Tamasin's interest in her welfare had become one.

'Do you think this is the sort of thing you might like to do when you stop swimming?' Tamasin had asked Nina at lunch the day before.

'If I'm any good at it,' she said as she picked the mushrooms out of her foccacia.

Tamasin had laughed.

'What's so funny?' Nina had asked.

'Oh Nina, you leave the office exhausted you're such a whirlwind of fantastic ideas. Then you say "if I'm any good". I thought a world record holder would have more confidence.'

'What does what I do in the water have to do with the ideas I have for the magazine? Or the photos I take? And what is the measure of a good photo or a good idea for a magazine? Swimming is completely different to that. I hit the wall first. That and only that makes me the best.' She looked up to find Tamasin staring at her. 'What?' she'd said before taking a bite.

'That is what Sam said you would say.'

'When?' Nina had asked.

'What do you mean, when?'

'When did you see Sam?'

Tamasin had started to say something, shaken her head, and then giggled.

Nina had sat back in her chair. 'No wonder the two of you have been asking so many questions about each other!' She'd clapped her hands. She couldn't imagine a more perfect couple. 'Since I am the topic of conversation, what else does he have to say?'

Tamasin had said nothing for a moment. 'Well, he tried to explain to me what your world was like. He uses the word "safe", which I find hard to imagine—competing against the best in the world is hardly what most of us would call safe.' She had picked at her salad while she thought. 'But I see what he means. Pushing yourself, physically, to the limit. Definite results, first, second and third. Precise. Thrilling. Big highs and lows. Lots of adrenaline. And lots of attention, of course.'

Nina had shrugged her shoulders. 'Bit like editing a magazine then,' she had offered. She liked talking to Tamasin so she had tried to explain. 'I think I live in a kind of fake world, Tam. People keep saying that sport gives you all this discipline and stuff and that it's good preparation for your life. But then you hear about a retired sportsperson who decides to make a comeback. And you think, why? What is out there that is so bad that you want to start doing all that training again, living with all that pressure, rather than just enjoying a nice life? Bit frightening really.'

'Maybe the nice life you imagine is kind of dull after all you have been through,' Tamasin had suggested.

'Maybe,' Nina had agreed. She had taken a sip of mineral water. 'Although I can't imagine sleeping in could ever be dull.' They had both laughed.

'You know, your swimming may have brought us together originally but you wouldn't keep getting asked to do things if you weren't good; if the diary entries you wrote for *sAssy* weren't entertaining, if the pictures weren't revealing, if the ideas you had had for this issue hadn't been interesting to our readers. We could have vetoed everything.'

'You might say that, but the person next to you will say I get the breaks because I am Nina Hallet.'

'Better make sure you hang out with people like me then,' Tamasin had told her.

Nina had looked across at the food hall jammed with lunchtime workers. 'Yeah, I guess,' she'd said before taking another bite from her foccacia.

*

Nina left the city offices of *sAssy* at top speed. It was a rare night off from training and she had a date. Well, technically, she didn't know if Nicholas considered it a date. When Nina learned he was rehearsing with the Sydney Youth Orchestra for three days in a building not far from the *sAssy* offices, she suggested they meet for dinner. And Nicholas had agreed.

'That's a great idea,' he had even said.

Nina zigzagged around all the people as they poured out of their offices on their way home. It made her feel quite alive to be part of the bustle of the crowds. She was usually in the water by this time of night, ploughing through two hundred metres of backstroke, one after another, until she thought she couldn't possibly move her arms to do one more lap. This was much more fun. The idea of meeting Nicholas in the city, surrounded by these well-dressed people who had just finished work for the day made her feel very grown up.

She began to get butterflies in her stomach as she approached the building where he was rehearsing. She held the fragment of paper with directions in one hand as she walked along looking for numbers.

Getting dressed that morning had taken forever. The dress code in the *sAssy* office reflected exactly what the magazine tried to portray. A group of young people dressing in the latest possible clothes. Nina had no trouble keeping up. In fact most of the clothes, thanks to her travels, were very well received. But today she had to wear something that might transfer into date wear. But not too much like date wear, because it wasn't really a date.

'Oh, Nicholas,' she sighed as she walked along. He was very confusing. As a supportive friend, she could not have asked for anything more. She had even let him see her 'go Nina go' decorations, as she called them. Where once she would have expected him to be a little dismissive of anything like that, he had just nodded as he stood in the middle of the room and slowly looking around.

'This is a good idea,' was all he said.

From then on the playful way he had always corrected Nina's grammar had taken on a new tone. It began one day when they were eating lunch together. Nina couldn't even re-member what she had been talking about when Nicholas had said, 'You have to stop that.'

'What?'

'The "what do I knows" and the "if I even win a medal" kind of stuff. I'd say you're subliminally sending negative mes-sages to your brain with statements like that.'

Nina couldn't believe what she was hearing. She had looked around behind him. Put her hand on his back in different places looking for a socket.

'Have you entered the matrix or something? Got yourself a new program?'

He'd smiled but he did not answer her. Eventually she was forced to be serious.

'I suppose you are right,' was all she could say.

'I usually am,' he'd responded casually. He was still smil-ing. She'd punched him in the shoulder.

'So, stop saying stuff like that,' he had added.

He had taken a bite of his sandwich. Nina had done the same. When he had finished his mouthful, he spoke again.

'In fact, every time you make one of those ridiculous statements your punishment will be saying ten times, very loudly, "Nicholas is always right, Nina is always wrong".'

Nina had nearly choked on her tomato when she heard that.

'Come on, I want to hear you practise. Repeat after me . . .'

Nina had hit him again. 'I'll follow you around repeating positive affirmations all day if you don't watch out,' she said.

'Good, better than that other crap,' he'd punched her back. But he had made his point. And she could still feel the touch of his hand on her arm.

*

'Five-fifty-six,' Nina said under her breath. 'This must be it.' She crossed the street. The entrance was an old-fashioned double door with big brass handles.

As soon as she entered the building she could hear the sound of instruments. Some warming up. Others in the middle of a tune. She laughed to herself. Imagine if Nicholas heard her call it 'a tune'. She moved to the stairs. She didn't know what she was going to say to him when she saw him.

'Stop this silliness,' she told herself. 'Just tell him about your day.'

She smiled as she passed others on the stairs. She continued to talk to herself. There was really no need to be nervous. He wouldn't have agreed to see her if he didn't want to. But this is the night, she concluded. The fantasies had to stop. The hours spent daydreaming about being his girlfriend. About holding his hand while waiting for her races at the Olympics.

'He was at the Olympic trials and never once did he even try to hold your hand.'

'Oh do shut up,' Nina muttered. She hated it when her

daydreams were interrupted by the voice. 'Well, he hasn't even tried to kiss you since the eisteddfod.'

'All right, all right,' she answered again. She'd have to give the voice a name one of these days she spent so much time in conversation with it. Anyway, she knew how to answer a challenge like that. Time. There was hardly a moment alone these days for herself, never mind for her and Nicholas. And besides, he really was shy.

'Yeah, right.' The voice again.

She reached the top landing and saw a large group of people, more like an orchestra, packing up their instruments. She poked her head around the door. There he was talking to another boy.

'Can I help you?' asked a man from behind the door, packing music sheets into a briefcase.

'Oh, um, I might be early, um, interrupting . . . I'm just here to meet a friend,' Nina fumbled.

'No, no, come in,' he told Nina. 'We've finished.'

'Nina!' Nicholas had spotted her at the door.

When she reached him, he introduced her to the boy he was talking to.

'Max, this is my good friend, Nina.'

Nina could tell Max was trying to work out where he had seen her before but he didn't say anything. Just the basic 'hello' and shook her hand.

For her part Nina was sure she was looking, just as intently, at him. He was beautiful. He was almost feline, if she had to use a word to describe him. She felt utterly tongue-tied. It occurred to her she had no trouble talking to the boys she swam with. Every girl she had ever met envied the close proximity she shared with the likes of Dominic, all of them wearing nothing more than a pair of swimmers. Yet she thought nothing of it. But put her around boys like the two she was standing next to and she couldn't string two words together. Just laugh ridiculously. And too loudly at that.

'Nice to meet you, Nina,' she heard him say. She nodded.

She looked at Nicholas. He was packing his satchel.

'I think I'll hang around with you more often,' she said, watching Max walk away. 'Wow!'

Nicholas looked back at Max. 'Not really my type,' he said. He grabbed his jacket from the back of the chair and wrapped it around his waist.

As Nicholas's words registered, a kaleidoscope of images tumbled through Nina's mind, like one of those postcards that kept unfolding and unfolding. In one instant everything made sense. How could she have been so blind?

She turned to Nicholas who seemed frozen on the spot, his jacket half tied around his waist, his face stricken as though he had said something he didn't mean to.

Nina swallowed hard. Hold it together, she thought, this is probably much harder for him than for you. She wanted to cry. She was sure she was in love with him. Be light, she told herself.

'As in, not your type of guy?' she heard herself ask. Her voice was too high she thought. A dead giveaway.

It took a moment for Nicholas to answer. Finally he nodded. He kept tying his jacket around his waist. 'Yeah.'

She took a deep breath. They looked at one another. She didn't know for how long.

'Are you okay with that?' she heard him ask softly.

'Yeah,' she heard herself say. Had she leant on the word too much? Tried to sound too okay? 'Of course,' she added.

He moved toward her. They embraced. They both burst into tears. Stood back from one another and then laughed. He wiped away her tears and she did the same for him. He grabbed her hand and kissed it. Like in an old-fashioned movie.

'Thanks,' he said. And they cried again.

'Alice knew?' Nina threw herself back in the chair. They were in a Spanish restaurant Nicholas knew of and were making fast work of a large paella.

'I must be the dumbest friend you have, Nicholas!'

'You've had a few more important things to worry about than who is doing what to whom in the schoolyard,' he reminded her.

They were having a good laugh. He had spent the last hour bringing her up to date with gossip that everyone at school—except Nina—seemed to know. She felt embarrassed that her feelings for Nicholas had gone on for so long. She wondered if it had given Shan and the girls even more to gloat about. She was so naive.

'Alice was the first to know, really. She was the one responsible for setting me up with my first boyfriend.' He thought for a moment. 'I guess you'd call him that. The first boy I liked, we'll say. We were at this band camp. Once she sensed it, she didn't give me a chance to think about it. She was onto it. She started us talking to one another in the way only Alice can.' They both laughed. Nina knew exactly what he meant. 'I guess it was her way of saying "it's cool",' he added

Thinking of Alice made her sad. Nicholas read her thoughts.

'She'll come round, Nina.'

'She won't talk to me. It's like she avoids me.'

'She's got her own stuff going on. Although that last chat you had didn't help.'

Nina shook her head. She didn't know what he meant.

'Well, I'm trying to convince her that you didn't say she was an embarrassment the night we went to the concert. That Shan was lying when she said you spoke to *Inside Sydney*. That, even though Shan's cousin works for the paper and swears it's the truth, you wouldn't say anything like that. And then the first time you guys have a decent talk you start going on about being on a diet. You are the last person who needs to

149

worry about stuff like that. Alice immediately assumed you were trying to make her feel like she should have a problem with her size.'

Nina couldn't believe what she was hearing. That wasn't what she meant. If only she could have explained herself to Alice properly. Tears came to her eyes. Would they ever stop?

'I'm such a terrible friend,' she dropped the crab claw from which she was trying to extract meat.

Nicholas moved around to Nina's side of the table. He sat in the chair next to her, put his arm around her shoulders. Nina resisted the hug.

'I'm all right,' she said. She knew her eyes were glistening but she willed the tears to stop. 'I should be giving you the hug.'

'I was worried about telling you,' he admitted.

Nina wiped her eyes with her serviette. She sat up straight. 'About Alice?' she hoped it sounded like she was teasing him.

He rolled his eyes. 'No, not about Alice.' He waited a moment. He didn't want to sound patronising. 'You've been under so much pressure lately. I didn't want to worry you with something else before the Olympics.'

'Oh, Nicholas.' She looked away, gathered herself. Stop being indulgent, she told herself. 'Do you really think I would let something like this bother me at the Olympics?' she challenged. She threw her serviette onto her plate.

He narrowed his eyes. The lines between his eyebrows crinkled. 'Good,' he said. 'I'm glad you feel like that because I need you to help me.' He took a deep breath. 'I need you to help me work out how to tell my dad.'

CHAPTER SEVENTEEN

GOLD FEVER GROWS

by Ron Samuels in the Olympic Village

Cape Town, Sunday. They're not saying much. After all, predictions have been made before. But there is a kind of fever at work in the Australian team headquarters at the Olympic Village. It gives everyone a golden glow. And anyone who ventures into the unashamedly green and gold halls comes away infected.

There has never been an Australian team as well prepared for an Olympic Games as this one. Twenty-five years of investment, in what is now a sports industry to rival any in the world, has brought us to this moment of truth. As in many areas of Australian life, we've always had the quality raw commodity. Just not the means, or perhaps the inclination, to turn it into a world class manufactured product. But Australian athletes, at these Games, look set to prove it can be done.

Traditionally, the swimmers carry our hopes. And around the pool there have never been more knowing nods, more satisfied smiles. No coach will say how many gold medals this team can win. But it boasts more world records than any team from Australia's so-called glory days.

Of all the swimmers, it is teenage favourite Nina Hallet who best embodies the history of Australian sport in her Olympic campaign.

She burst onto the international scene with all the promise of a country awash with the health and energy of post-war youth. She's held onto her Olympic dream as cheats, bribes and corruption have done their best to taint it. And she has emerged as a young woman with a cool head, quietly determined to take on the world and honour the Olympic ideal in the only way she knows how.

The dark days for Australian sport, and for Nina Hallet, are well and truly behind us. Bring on the Games.

Nina sat in the overstuffed armchair at Australian head-quarters, watching the clock. If she were caught here—rather than in her room—by one of her coaches she would be in deep trouble. On the afternoon before her first Olympic final she should be sleeping.

But she had four slips of yellow paper in her hand. Each a message from Nicholas. He had called on the half hour for the last two hours.

The phone rang. Nina leant forward in her chair, ready to take the call in the common room. Brenda, the woman who had team headquarters totally under control, looked at Nina as she answered it. She had talked to Nicholas on each occasion. She shook her head. Nina fell back into the chair.

She hoped Nicholas was calling with good news. Her advice was to tell his father. She understood his reluctance, even though, apparently, Nina's conversation with Mr Coulter in the car had been the catalyst to a new relationship between the two.

'He came back to the hospital after taking you home and just talked and talked. Said he loved music but he couldn't encourage me because he didn't want me to suffer the same disappointment. But he realised he'd been a fool. He'd pushed Mum away but he wasn't going to do it a second time. I'd always thought I was the reason she left,' he told Nina. 'You know, too odd!'

But now Nicholas worried that revealing he was gay would put too much strain on the tentative friendship.

Nina's argument was to get it all out in the open. A relationship based on half-truths was only half a relationship. If he lost his father because of that then he wasn't that much of a father, she had argued. Nicholas had agreed but every time there was the opportunity to talk to his father he had let it pass.

'Didn't seem like the right time,' he would say.

'Remind me to tell the Starter that will you,' she had finally told him. He didn't know what she was talking about. 'When I line up to start a final at the Olympics remind me that I can call over to him and say, "excuse me, doesn't feel right for me today, can we come back tomorrow?".'

'Nina,' Brenda's voice broke her thoughts. She ran over to one of the common phones as Brenda transferred Nicholas through.

'We didn't see it. How'd you go?' she heard him ask. Nicholas and his dad were on holiday together on the northern New South Wales coast.

'Okay. Lane three.'

'Good.' There was a pause. 'And?'

She had finally told him about the magic feeling. 'Hasn't appeared.'

'It will, Nina. Just forget about it now. You're worrying too much.' Nina smiled at his 'firm' voice. 'Clearly you don't need it,' he added. 'You're in an Olympic final!'

'Yeah,' she hoped he was right.

'How are you feeling?'

'Sick.' She had to be honest.

'Yeah, I can imagine. But, it's going to be great. *You're* going to be great, Nina.'

She nodded without replying. She didn't know what to say. 'I've got to go soon though. Get some sleep.'

'Of course, I'll let you go.'

'Nicholas!' she couldn't contain herself any longer.

'Yeah?'

'Well?'

'Yes!' She could hear elation in his voice.

'You told him?'

'Yeah.'

153

'And?' She shook her head. Speak, for goodness sake.

'Everything is fine,' he said. 'I think it's going to be, anyway.'

Nina wasn't sure what that meant. 'Nicholas . . .'

'Nina, it's going to work out. But I don't want you to worry about it for now. You've got enough going on. Are you listening to me?'

'Yes . . .'

'I just want to say you're more powerful than you know. Remember that when you stand up for the final tonight. Okay?'

'Okay,' was all she could say.

He wished her luck again and they said their goodbyes. Nina gently put the receiver back in its cradle. She would do as he said. She was ready to sleep.

*

She noticed her nails as she removed her T-shirt, the last piece of clothing, before she turned around to face the final of the 100m Backstroke. Nothing was left of them. She had bitten them all off in the marshalling room. She rubbed the tops of her fingers against her swimsuit. She wished she could rub away her nerves. She'd never bitten her nails before.

'I don't know how to do this.'

That thought again. It had first entered her mind in the small airless room where the finalists were marshalled. She remembered Jebby's words: 'The Olympics are like nothing else'.

'I don't know how to do this.'

'Yes, you do,' she told herself. 'Be tough,' she instructed.

Nina bent down to steady herself on the plastic box that now contained her clothes. She could see her green and gold trainers. She urged the colours to do something. Embolden her. Help her to keep her mind on the job. But they lay lifeless in the cold box that would be removed from the pool deck in a moment, to be collected after the race.

'When you are the Olympic champion,' she whispered. Concentrate, Ninja. She hated that nickname. Why was she using it now?

'Why are you thinking these things?' she whispered again.

The whistle blew. It was time to go. She took a deep breath. She stood up.

'When you turn around the only thing you will think about is swimming this race,' she told herself. 'Block all other sound out.'

She turned. But an Australian team chant broke her concentration. She walked as fast as she could to the edge of the pool and jumped in.

Later, Nina would say there was no time to think. From the moment she came back to the surface everything had been a rush. The crouch to start, the take your mark, the gun. Not a second to steady herself. To get a rhythm. To even be part of the race.

She was halfway down the first lap before she realised the commands she was giving to her body were all a contradiction. One second it would be 'spin your arms, get on top of the water, keep up down the first fifty'. The next second it would be 'steadily, Nina, steadily'.

She hit the turn. With a grunt, she thrust her body through the flutter kick. It was that uncharacteristic noise that did it. For when she came out of the turn, Nina had the sensation of her mind and body coming together for the first time that evening. As though each had decided she'd been played with enough for one night. Nina suddenly found herself in the middle of a swimming race. She said thank you to whoever was responsible.

But what damage did she have to make up? She moved her eyes left and right. With less than fifty metres to go she was not in front but she wasn't far off. She was at the shoulder of American, Andrea Kratzman, who was in lane four, right next to Nina. Ulrike Stodt from the Netherlands, further over in lane five, was with them. And in lane seven, Nina had a sense of Rose Manning being close as well.

She had no time to waste. If she was going to make it up from here, she had about thirty-five metres to do it. She had to make every stroke count. And she had to ignore the pain. It would be worse if she was beaten.

Fade, she implored the others. And they seemed to respond. She drew level to Kratzman. Forget them. Swim your own race. She could hear the crowd. She could hear her body. Keep kicking, she reminded herself. Her legs felt thick and heavy. She was breathing hard. But she was stroke for stroke with Kratzman. She was sure Stodt was there. Didn't know about the others.

Suddenly the flags were above her. Four strokes to go. She pushed all the energy she had into those long, laboured strokes. She lunged for the wall with a wrenching yell.

Nina reached for the rope. Missed. Went under the water and reached for it again. She was sure it was there. Somewhere. She found it and hung on to it until she got her breath back.

Everyone was cheering. The Australians included. But Kratzman was jumping up beside Nina, punching the air. Nina understood she hadn't won before she looked at the scoreboard. But what had happened? Her name was second. She had made it in before Stodt. Only eight hundredths of a second separated the three of them.

Nina didn't know what to feel. She hadn't beaten her best time. But Kratzman hadn't beaten Nina's best time either. Nina felt some relief. Her world record still stood.

'Good race,' Kratzman reached for Nina's hand before she knew what was going on.

'Yeah,' Nina gathered herself. 'Congratulations,' she added. She hated saying the words but it was the right thing to do.

'You too,' Andrea said before jumping out over the end of the pool and shoving both her arms in the air in a victory sign. The crowd roared.

Nina exited the pool in the more traditional way. She congratulated Ulrike Stodt as they both floated over to the ladder at the side of the pool. When Nina followed the bronze medallist out of the pool, the roar came again. She stood and raised her arm in appreciation of the show of support. The Australians started singing, 'Way to go, Nina. Way to go'.

As she made her way across the pool deck to prepare for the medal presentation, Nina saw her mother and father in the stands. Their arms were raised high. Waving madly at her. Jumping as they waved. She stopped for a moment and waved back. She wondered how they felt. Were they just acting excited to show her they weren't disappointed in her? Was a silver medal enough? They seemed happy with her.

As she moved on she was struck by another thought. She had just won a silver medal at the Olympic Games, in a race that for a moment she thought she had blown completely. But she hadn't. She had got herself back together and finished second.

'The Olympic games are like no other,' Jebby had said.

Now Nina knew what she meant. She had been distracted, that's all. But she had made it to the Games and already there was a silver medal to show for it. And there was still one race to go.

Nina felt excited. More excited than she had felt for a long time. As she exited the pool deck, she made a promise. She promised herself that no matter what, she would not be distracted again.

*

Nina jumped as arms came around her from behind and a kiss landed on her cheek.

'Hello love,' she heard her mum say.

'What are you reading,' her father asked as he put his arm around her shoulder and gave her a hug.

It was a silly question. They stood in front of a giant pin board on the wall of the Australian team headquarters. It was quickly being filled with press clippings detailing the successes of the Australian team at these Cape Town Olympics. Nina pointed to the couple of stories about her 100m Backstroke swim.

'Everyone is being really nice to me,' she told her parents. 'The papers, all the herogrammes and stuff. L-EV8 Sportswear has sent flowers and all sorts of things.'

'And so they should,' her mother said. 'You've won your first medal for your country at the Olympics.'

'"Proving she is not a spent force in swimming, Hallet stormed home in the dying stages of the final of the 100m Backstroke to clinch her first Olympic medal, a silver for Australia,"' her father read aloud from one of the cuttings on the wall. He laughed. 'Spent force, eh Nina! You showed them, love.' He gave her another hug.

Nina decided this was the time. She revealed a black velvet box that she had kept by her side. 'Check this out.' She handed the box to her father.

It had been taken from her for engraving on the night that she won the silver medal. It had been returned just in time for her mum and dad's visit to the athlete's village.

Her father looked at Nina before standing next to her mother to open the box. Her mother's eyes were filled with tears. A smile and lots of nodding was about all she could manage. Her father managed to say 'good girl' before he too was overcome.

Nina laughed at them.

'Hopeless,' she said and they all laughed again. 'Imagine what you'll be like when I get the real one!'

'This is the real one, Nina.' Her mother was onto her meaning straight away. She handed her daughter back her prize.

Nina rolled her eyes. But she wouldn't take the medal. 'I want you to have it,' was all she said before leading them out of headquarters for a short tour of the village. It had been enough of an ordeal to get them a two hour visitors' pass. She wasn't about to waste it.

'Nina!' her mother called as they followed her down the flight of stairs. They emerged on Athletes Boulevard, the main thoroughfare through the accommodation quarters of the village. From there they could catch a shuttle bus to anywhere within the massive compound.

'We need to talk about this,' her mother said as they caught up to her.

'This is where we get the bus.' Nina looked down the boulevard to see if a bus was coming, avoiding eye contact with her mother. 'I thought I might show you the ent-cent as everyone is calling it. Every entertainment you could possibly imagine. It's like a mall.'

'Hey Nina,' a voice called from across the road. Nina looked over to see the Australian kayaker Dale Hamilton. 'Congratulations.'

'Thanks, Dale.'

'It'll be gold on Saturday, you know.'

'I know,' she called back.

'Good on ya,' he waved as he walked into his building.

She looked back to her parents and found her mother about to speak.

'There is no point pretending the race isn't going to happen, Mum. It is.'

'But it doesn't matter . . .'

'It does matter,' Nina stopped her. 'I've come all this way

and I've got to win this. We've all worked too hard to get here.'

She stopped for a moment. It wasn't even about that. How could she explain it?

'Look, I was scared before. I'd forgotten about the thrill of just standing up and giving it a go with nothing to lose. Because it seems like I have so much to lose now. But what is the worst that can happen? I might not win but I'm not going to, like, die. Am I?' She looked away from her parents. The worry in their eyes was almost too much to bear. She sounded more on top of things than she truly felt but that wasn't the point. The more she kept talking like this the easier it got.

'So, look. I'm going in there safe in the knowledge that I am the world record holder. That gives me a bit of an advantage, wouldn't you say? I have nothing to lose. Just do my best. And race the others. And see what happens. And when I think of it like that, then I get really excited. I can't wait for Saturday to come around. Everywhere around me Australians are winning gold medals and I've got another chance. I just can't wait to give it a go.' She shrugged her shoulders and smiled. 'Does that sort of make sense?'

The bus pulled up beside them as she finished. She stood to one side to allow her parents to get on first. Her mother squeezed Nina's shoulder and smiled before getting on the bus. Her father followed, grabbing onto the railing beside the door to steady himself. He leaned in toward his daughter.

'Sounds like a pretty good plan to me,' he said as he made his way into the vehicle.

*

If she thought her new attitude was going to stop her from feeling nervous in the days she had to wait before the 200m Backstroke, she was mistaken. Her fingernails didn't stand a chance.

She and Jake got on better than she could remember. He had become a better traveller. With that under control his enthusiasm for everything the village had to offer helped Nina see things she might have missed in the all-consuming attempt to win a gold medal. More than once he would give her a nudge in the ribs and point to something out the bus window. One day it was the men's basketball team from India. Seven slim men at least two metres tall—without shoes. With the brightly coloured turbans they each wore on their heads, they were the tallest men Nina had ever seen. Walking together, in time, Nina was reminded of elegant, loping creatures like giraffes striding across the African plains. Only in the athlete's village, the plains were replaced by the quadrangle known as the International Zone.

Jake was able to enjoy all the Olympics had to offer. And he still swam personal best times in his events, the 200m Breaststroke and 400m Individual Medley.

'If I can do best times, so can you,' was all he had said to her as they shared a post-finals bowl of ice-cream the night before her 200m Backstroke. She had looked at him as he sat with his feet up on the chair next to him. There were days she thought she might be able to like him as more than a friend. Then other days, when he could be completely irritating, she knew it could never work.

*

Nina relaxed back into her seat as she travelled to the pool for the final of the 200m Backstroke. She had qualified in lane four. Right where she wanted to swim. She felt as powerful as Declan Sinclair's handshake. She had run into her old friend the day before, in the cafeteria.

'Mind if I sit with you, Nina Hallet?' she had heard a deep English voice ask.

It turned out that he had followed her progress over the

years and knew that she'd won a silver medal a few nights before.

'And how do you feel about that?' He was eating a mountain of pasta for his lunch while Nina picked at a sandwich.

She wasn't worried about letting Declan down, so she could be honest with him. 'I'm trying not to dwell on it, if that's what you mean.'

He had nodded. 'Good.' He seemed to drink half a bottle of water in one gulp. 'There is no point. This is a new race and nothing else matters. It's going to take every ounce of experience you have, Nina. I'm going to enjoy watching you win.'

He had left her alone after shaking her hand.

'How are you feeling, Nina?' Rose Manning broke into her thoughts. Rose had failed to make the final but was going to the pool early to catch up with her parents before the night's swimming began.

'Good thanks,' Nina answered. She had not bothered to befriend Rose during the time they were Olympic teammates. Some other time, Nina thought.

'Do you think you can beat Andrea Kratzman? She looked pretty good in the heats.'

Nina looked at the girl, trying to make sure she had heard her correctly. She looked at her coach Eric Anderson. He had his eye on Rose as well, trying to work out exactly what she was talking about.

'Not that it matters; I don't have to race her. She just looked good to me.'

'Shut up, Rose.' Both Eric and Nina spoke together.

Nina was out the door the moment the bus pulled into the pool entrance. Unlike the night of the 100m final, she felt as though she knew what she was doing. She breathed in the big, wide, white pool deck. The overbright lights. How she'd been looking forward to this moment!

She stripped off and was into the pool for her warm up

before anyone else. She pulled her goggles down over her eyes and swung her arms high to execute an exaggerated, over-arched dive into the water. Her fingertips broke the glassy surface. With that entry the last piece of the puzzle fell into place. She had forgotten about it for a few days. Trained herself to forget about it, she had to admit. But she didn't have to forget about it anymore.

She surfaced, letting out such a loud shriek that Eric looked around from the conversation he was having with another coach to see if anything was wrong. All he saw was Nina rolling around in the water, lying on her back, performing a double-armed backstroke before disappearing under the water. He thought she was just loosening up. He didn't realise it was Nina's imitation of an acrobat doing cartwheels, one after the other, no hands. An interpretation in water, per-formed by a girl who had found her magic.

*

The whistle brought all eight girls in the water up to the wall together. Nina gripped the handles on either side of the block and brought her feet up to the wall. They landed on the yellow starting pad.

'Take your mark'.

She pulled up with her arms and crouched into position. But something felt wrong. She scrunched her toes up, trying to get comfortable. For some reason the balls of her feet didn't want to hold her in the usual position. Had she placed her feet too high on the pad? Too low? It was an instinctive thing, not something she usually had to think about. She pulled in harder with her arms. But that only made the angle steeper. Did she look down at her feet? Go early? False start? A thou-sand thoughts in a split second. The gun went. Too late. Just go. Explode, she told herself. She let the handgrips go. Flung her arms back. But her feet had nothing to push off. One

163

slipped right down the wall. The other followed. And so did Nina.

The other girls shot out from the wall, down the pool, on their way in the final of the 200m Backstroke for Women. But Nina was on her way to the bottom of the pool. Bubbles flew past her in the opposite direction. She didn't know what had happened. Had the other girls gone? Had the Starter called a false start? She hadn't heard a second gun. Get to the surface, she screamed. Her arms did something. She didn't know what. Whatever it took to get to the top. Kick, she told her legs. She surfaced alone. The race had begun. It had started without her. No false start.

'Oh my god,' was her first conscious thought. She realised she was too far from the wall to get any push-off from it. She gave the mightiest kick she could force from her body. She spun her arms. Anything to get some momentum. Forget race plans. Just fly. Catch up. At least try. That was the only thing she could think of to do.

CHAPTER EIGHTEEN

NINA THOUGHT SHE had imagined every possible scenario when it came to outcomes of a swimming race. It wasn't even that she had to imagine. In her career she had been a winner. She had been a loser. But in her wildest nightmares she'd never imagined this.

For a moment it might not have been that bad. There was a race to swim. A chance to catch up. Give the best backstroke swimmers in the world a few seconds start and still beat them. What a story that would have been!

But there had been no miracle. No superhuman effort. She had heard stories of the body performing amazing feats in the face of incredible odds. But not her body. She had made her way through the field only to fade in the dying stages of the race. She hit the wall, exhausted. Defeated. Her chance for redemption had passed.

At first, she behaved in the way that she should. She congratulated the winner—Andrea Kratzman again. She smiled as they shook hands.

'Did you slip?' the hearty American voice put into words, for the first time, Nina's shame. She shrugged it off. Nodded.

'Too bad,' Kratzman added. The pity behind the words made her want to throw up. But Nina kept it together. Ignored the insults the voice in her head was hurling her way.

And as she said to the press, there was always next time. She was young. She would be back to avenge her loss. She didn't need anyone to feel sorry for her.

*

Nina had managed to avoid speaking to Chris Baxter, one of the team psychologists, after the Olympics. It had been easy to do. The athlete's village was a big place.

When Nina returned to Sydney there was schoolwork to catch up on. She was in Year 11 after all. And there was swimming training. Usually, she would have taken a break after a major swimming event. It didn't seem appropriate this time. She had to prove she was serious about making up for a mistake like the one she had made in Cape Town.

But more importantly, what was there to talk about? Other people had had far worse things happen to them. Parents divorced. Fathers lost jobs. Mothers died. All that she had done, she kept telling herself, was slip in a stupid swimming race.

But nothing that she did could stop the video replay that ran over and over again in her head. Nothing that she said answered the questions that tumbled over in her mind, day after day. How did it happen? What had she done? How could it have turned out like this?

She tried to forget about it. Move forward. Stay in the present. But that wasn't any better. Everywhere she went people wanted to talk about the Olympics, about a new era in world sport where Australians were once again dominant. About the spoils of victory. Everywhere there was evidence of what Nina's life might have been. If she had been a winner. If she had done her job. If she had performed one of the basic requirements of an athlete—never mind one that was supposed to be a professional—and got off to a good start. It didn't even have to be good. Just vaguely competent.

She couldn't sleep. She couldn't eat. When she did eat, it wasn't stuff that would make anyone's list of recommended dietary requirements.

Chris had been phoning the house from the day Nina got home from Cape Town. Nina was given the messages. But she refused to return the calls. One day she answered the phone to hear Chris's voice on the other end. Nina agreed to see her. She didn't know why. Anything to get them off her back, she reasoned.

'Are you sure it was pity?' Chris asked.

'Of course it was pity. What else?' Nina couldn't help the words spitting from her mouth. The psychologist didn't answer. Nina had come to the meeting determined to say nothing. But these silences were infuriating. She felt impelled to talk.

'Like when I got out of the pool and the crowd clapped,' she challenged.

It was a moment that would not go away. After she had completed her duty at the end of the race and congratulated the medal winners, she had bolted across the lane ropes to the first ladder she spotted. In her desperation to get out she had found herself on the side that required her to walk all the way across the breadth of the pool deck before she could make her escape under the grandstand. She had had to walk in front of the thousands of people who had been there to see her incompetence. As soon as she lifted herself out of the pool the crowd had begun to clap. Nina had realised how far she had to walk. Then the Australians in the crowd had stood and cheered. She had frozen, not knowing what to do. She didn't want anyone to clap. She didn't want anyone to even acknowledge her presence.

'What else could it be? The pathetic world record holder who couldn't cut it when it came to the big event.' She didn't look at Chris as she spoke. 'And then at school, the first day back, the same thing.'

She had made her way along the overgrown path as she had done every morning she had been at Harper. When she emerged a group of students was waiting for her. As soon as they saw her they had stood and clapped and whistled. She was dumbstruck. She didn't know what to do. She had wanted to run away. But that seemed childish. Instead she had barrelled through the group, heading for the quadrangle and assembly. But they had wanted to shake her hand. She could have strangled Nicholas. He was the only one who knew she would come back on that day.

'Nina, do you think it's possible that these people were clapping you out of respect?'

Chris was sitting on the couch where the two of them had started. Nina, after some pacing, had ended up in the back corner of the room, one shoulder against the wall.

'Respect!'

Nina couldn't believe what she was hearing. She knew the kind of respect people had for her. Her mother had made that clear when Nina met them outside the pool in Cape Town. Her parents had been in the grandstand to witness the race. They had waited a long time to see her. The first thing her mother had said was, 'what happened'? But she hadn't given Nina a chance to respond before adding, 'the man sitting beside us said you weren't concentrating'.

Nina had not known what to say. What man? What would he know? But then, maybe she could have concentrated better? Her mother had kept talking but Nina didn't hear a word she said. She had wanted to look at her father. Tell him she was concentrating. Tell him she didn't know what had happened. Tell him she was so sorry. Sorry he had wasted all that time on her, all those early mornings, training sessions, swimming meets. Sorry he had given up his time only for her to throw it away. But she hadn't been able to look at him.

'Respect for what exactly?' she asked from her corner.

'You.'

'Oh, please!' If Nina could have pushed herself into the wall she would have, just to get away from the thought.

'You swam an amazing race. A thrilling race. You had the

entire crowd thinking for a moment that you might actually catch everyone up.'

'But, I didn't.'

'No, but you gave it a go. You didn't give up. You came fifth in the final at the Olympics. And you won a silver medal only a few days before.'

'Yeah, right! Silver! Like, whacko,' she twirled her index finger upward in the air.

'What does that mean, Nina?'

Nina took a moment to answer. 'Well, you know what they say, Chris.'

The psychologist could hardly hear Nina as she spoke. She leant across the back of the couch to catch Nina's muffled words. But she didn't need to. Nina looked straight at her for the first time during the session and repeated the words, loudly.

'Second is first of the losers.'

*

Although Nina had made another appointment to see Chris Baxter she never went back. Summer was around the corner. Things would get better.

She decided to take a long break from swimming. Enjoy her life. Be a teenager. Get ready for her final year at school. Everyone thought it was a good idea. But that left her with more spare time. More time to think. More time at home.

The only thing she could actually concentrate on were the romance novels she found, by chance, in a bargain basement book sale. The author's name was Harriet Ray Walker. Her heroines were always modern, magnificent creatures who weathered setbacks only to find true love and the perfect career.

Her mother hated the books. Hated Nina wasting her mind. So Nina started to ride her bike again. Took her book. Found somewhere to sit. A park swing, a bench down at the bay. And read.

Sometimes her other self caught up with her. People would ask her if she was Nina Hallet. Sometimes people would say nice things. Sometimes not so nice. One day she was polite to a boy riding a skateboard only to have him tell his friend she was 'that chick who choked at the Olympics'.

So she began to deny who she was. Most people were not insistent. She didn't think she looked like Nina Hallet. No sleep and a poor diet were making sure of that. She wore her hair long. Carried a skipper hat and put it on as soon as she took off her bike helmet.

One rainy afternoon she had no choice but to find an indoor venue to do her reading. She rode to a small mall about five kilometres from Harper Bay, called Willow Way. Nina always wondered how such an ugly mall could have sprung from such a pretty name. In the mall there was an even uglier cafe. It had orange plastic chairs and Formica tables and smelt of oil that had cooked too many batches of chips. But it was clean. She was sure no one would notice her in there.

Less than ten minutes after Nina sat down, Sharon Little walked in. Nina didn't see her until the other girl was standing over her.

'Didn't expect to find you here,' Nina heard.

She looked up to find Sharon lighting a cigarette. A packet of cigarettes was thrown down on the table. The lighter followed. Sharon sat down in the chair opposite Nina.

Nina had no desire to talk and she didn't want Sharon to see the book she was reading. She closed the book under the table and left it on her lap. She leant back on the legs of her chair and looked at the other girl. She didn't seem to be in a hurry to leave.

'Didn't expect to find you here, either.' Nina couldn't think of anything else to say.

The woman who worked behind the counter of the shop brought Sharon a black coffee. It was the stalest coffee Nina had ever smelt.

'It'll keep me going 'til I get something stronger,' Sharon said, as though in answer to Nina's thoughts. 'Not at swimming training?'

Nina shook her head. 'Thought I'd have a bit of a break.'

'Live a little,' the other girl said as she stirred half a teaspoon of sugar into the coffee.

Nina nodded.

Sharon was about to take a sip of coffee when she hesitated. Instead she pushed the packet of cigarettes and the lighter over to Nina.

'Want one?'

After a moment, Nina took the offering and Sharon went back to her coffee. 'We're going to the Bay Room tonight.'

Nina nodded again. The Bay Room was part of the local RSL. Nina had heard a lot of stories. Not any that would make her want to go to a place like that. 'Isn't it Friday Night Frenzy?' Still, she wanted to prove she wasn't completely out of touch. She pulled a cigarette out of its packet. She had no idea what to do with it after that.

Sharon nodded as she put her coffee cup down on its saucer. She looked at the cigarette, looked at Nina. She smiled, raising her eyebrows at the same time. 'Wanna come?'

*

Sharon taught Nina how to light a cigarette and how to drink bourbon and coke.

From then on Nina didn't need much help. She did the rest all by herself. It didn't take long for her to push away all the people she needed so badly. Jake had been easy to get rid of.

'He was so available,' she heard herself tell anyone who

might be listening. 'Always has been, even though I never asked him to be.'

In those moments, bolstered by a drink or two, she could pretend that she had behaved well. Only when she was alone did the real story taunt her.

Jake had sat by the pool the night of her Olympic race and waited for Nina to complete her post-race swim down. He waited for her while she changed into dry clothes and escorted her from the pool to where her mum and dad were waiting for her. When he held the heavy glass door at the pool exit open for Nina, she walked through but not without comment. 'I'm not completely useless, you know,' she hurled at him. Jake passed it off as Nina being hurt.

But that moment gave Nina all the latitude she needed and she took it. The harder Jake tried, the ruder she was to him. He came to her house one day to play her a song he had recorded with his new songwriting partner. Jake used the money he earned from swimming to equip himself with a small recording studio at his house.

It wasn't that Nina didn't like the song. On the contrary it was so good that it threw her into a rage. Mostly at herself for throwing away all the opportunities she had been given. For not doing anything good for so long. For not doing anything she could be even remotely proud of. But instead of these thoughts motivating her to do something about herself, she attacked Jake. She knew from the look in his eyes she had gone too far.

'You know, I don't have to take this crap from you,' Jake said quietly as he took the CD from the machine and packed up his belongings.

'No? Then how come you keep coming back for more?' Nina challenged.

'I dunno,' Jake shrugged his shoulders. 'Thought it might help. But I can see you're doing just fine without me.' His voice was still soft, controlled. No sign of sarcasm. He hoisted his bag over his shoulder.

'Yeah, I am, thanks very much,' Nina's shrill voice was in direct contrast to her friend's.

'Bye, Nina,' Jake said as he walked out of her house without even a backward glance.

Nicholas had never been available to Nina. The battles she fought with him were all in her own head. While he would have been happy to keep her close she didn't seem to need him. She hardly spoke to him. She couldn't. Couldn't look at him, stand next to him. She could only imagine what he thought of her. She ached when she looked at him. Beautiful Nicholas.

As the months went by and she dug herself further and further into her hole, he shone. He became golden. And beside him she felt more and more shabby. Not worthy of his company. What an embarrassment she must have been to him.

She told herself she didn't care. Didn't care about swimming. Didn't care about Jake. Didn't care about Nicholas. Didn't care about the way she looked, the way she felt. She didn't care about anything.

'How could you let yourself go like this,' her mother would yell. It had taken Annette Hallet a long time to crack. Even Nina had to admit that. A dog had been the first attempt to take Nina's mind off that night at the Olympics. Then talking. Nina didn't think she could rehash, one more time, the months before the Olympics. Jack leaving. The decision not to go to the Institute of Sport. Stay with Chip. To stay at school. To talk to the press, to not talk to the press.

The rehashing led to recriminations. Each blaming the other for something. There would be an apology. A brief truce. Then it would start again. Until there was only yelling.

When Nina started staying out, getting drunk, restrictions

were enforced. Where once there had been trust, now there were curfews and groundings.

'What do you want from me,' Nina would scream back. 'I'm sorry that I am not the perfect daughter you expected.'

'I never expected you to be perfect, Nina,' her mother was almost shaking as they faced each other in the kitchen. It was four in the morning. Nina's mother had, once again, been waiting for Nina to come home. 'But I didn't expect a drunk. And neither did your father. You disgust him, the way you've been carrying on.'

'Fine,' Nina declared, holding back the tears. She hadn't been able to face her father since the night of the slip. She had disgusted him for the last time. 'Tomorrow I'll move out and you'll never have to watch me disgust you again.'

Nina found herself a one-bedroom apartment hardly bigger than the room she had lived in at her parents' house. It was the first apartment she looked at, in the first real estate agency she walked into. It had pink walls and brown carpet and the tenants before had been smokers, too.

She sat on the living room floor on that first afternoon with a large packet of salt and vinegar chips, a bottle of cola and a packet of cigarettes.

All she could think was, what am I doing here? All she really wanted was to go home.

CHAPTER NINETEEN

NINA SPENT A moment deciding which chair in the mall would give her the best angle of the billboard. In the end she crossed the empty street and crouched down against the window of a jewellery shop. She was further away than she wanted to be but at least she wouldn't break her neck from the strain of looking up.

The billboard was massive, the largest in the inner city. It was an advertisement for a clothing store that had been around forever but was trying to reinvent itself. It wasn't the clothes that interested Nina so much as the campaign itself. A young Australian photographer called Eve Madison, who'd made a name for herself in Europe, had been brought home to shoot the campaign.

Nina had met her once, years ago, when her swimming had first made her famous. She had gone to a photographer's studio not far from where the billboard stood. A great white warehouse with exposed wood beams, oversized furniture, and a tall, rake-thin photographer's assistant, called Eve, with the most fantastic shock of flame-red, spiky hair Nina had ever seen. Eve told Nina that she was on her way to London the week after the shoot. Nina doubted Eve would remember her. But she'd been looking out for her work ever since.

'Hey darlin', take a photo of me!'

An impeccably coiffured drag queen had spotted the camera around Nina's neck. With a fake feather boa wound around her outstretched arms, and red-sequinned platform shoes elevating an already impressive pair of legs, Nina felt dwarfed by the creature in front of her. A tiny red-sequinned mini-dress and red wig made up the ensemble. Nina slid right down onto the ground to take a picture that would make her model look as tall as the buildings around her. She had used almost an entire roll of film by the time the drag queen had performed all her poses.

'Are you all right, darlin'?' she asked as Nina changed the roll.

'Yeah,' Nina answered as she wound on the film.

Suddenly the long limbs were folded away to bring the drag queen down on her haunches in front of Nina. 'Hmm,' she said, not entirely satisfied. 'You look tired, doll. Don't stay here for long, okay? Too many lunatics around these days.' She fished a card from a black patent leather tote on the ground beside her. 'I'm over there at Rocco's,' she pointed across the square. 'I do a show at midnight and at two o'clock. You need anything, see Eric on the door and ask for Lana. Got it?'

Nina took the card. 'Got it. Thanks.'

Lana was up and on her way across the square before she stopped with a pirouette. 'Actually, you should come in one night and be our official backstage photographer,' she called.

'But I could never bring enough film,' Nina yelled back.

Lana threw her head back with a whoop. 'Come anyway,' she said as she pranced off.

Nina watched Lana, hips and feather boa swaying from side to side as she parted the small crowd waiting outside the club. A sparkling red star in her own nocturnal world. Nina wondered if Lana, like her, waited all day for night to come.

Nina leant her head back on the glass shop window. There was more of Eve Madison's work in the windows of the city store and she wanted to look at them tonight. But she was getting tired. Lana was right. There were lunatics around but not, as the drag queen suggested, on the street. They were living in the flat above Nina's. The man seemed to come home every night just to yell. For hours and hours. Then in the morning it would be the woman's turn; only the noise she made was more in line with a high-pitched bellow. And in between all that there was incessant vacuuming. It was one of the reasons Nina had set out on her after-hours meandering in the first place.

Within a short time, though, it had become a ritual. Armed with her camera she had begun to amass a pictorial essay of the night-time extremes of the city. Lana would be one of the more colourful entries.

Nina got up and moved through the slowly gathering groups of people, all waiting to get into clubs and bars along the strip. She cleared the crowds and made her way toward the city, stretched out her arms, threw her head back, and closed her eyes just for a second. How she loved the inky, concealing, darkness of night. Nina felt as though she was draped in a silky black velvet cape that made her invisible to all.

'"Come, gentle night; come, loving, black-browed night,"' she recited as she walked along the footpath. She stopped as she spotted a handsome businessman on the other side of the road. He was sitting on his briefcase, slowly inhaling a ciga-rette as he coveted a midnight blue Ferrari from behind the shop window. 'Bring me my Romeo,' Nina giggled to herself as she brought the lens to her eye and captured the dreamer. 'God you're pathetic, Hallet,' she told herself.

She looked over the top of her camera at her subject. He was lost in another world. She witnessed something like it almost every evening. Just a few nights before she'd come across an office worker, a woman, sitting on a street bench, completely exhausted. Her high heels were off and she was massaging her feet. But when she saw the man she was meeting, a complete transformation took place right in front of Nina's eyes. Everything was abandoned; bag, briefcase, shoes, even the exhaustion of the day as she ran toward him. They had literally leapt into one another's arms. Nina was very pleased with the series of photos she had caught.

She crossed the park and found herself in front of the clothing store she was seeking and again in front of the work of Eve Madison. Looking at the full-sized window banners, Nina wondered if she had that ability, the eye for detail, the originality and the sensitivity to bring her subjects alive in the way Eve Madison obviously could. Nina thought of Tamasin. She had once thought highly of Nina's work. She wondered what the magazine editor thought of her now. 'Just call her,' a voice said from somewhere inside her head.

'Hmm,' she sighed out loud. Maybe she would. In the morning. She yawned. She had to get home. Get a little sleep before the yelling and the vacuum cleaner made it impossible.

She put her camera away and grabbed a bottle of water from her bag. But as she stood and turned in the direction of the bus stop, something made her look up.

'Damn,' she said as tears came to her eyes.

There was Dominic in glorious black and white, his Olympic gold medal draped across his bare chest, the new face for a telecommunications company. Nina didn't know how long she stood there looking at her old friend but eventually it started to get light. She walked on. Eve Madison was a distant memory.

CHAPTER TWENTY

NINA KEPT HER head down as she paid for her gum. A pile of magazines was sitting right there on the counter. Everywhere she went it was the same.

'**Come Home Nina—A Mother's Misery**' the headline read.

Underneath the headline were three photos of Nina. The first as a beaming, innocent fourteen-year-old on the night she was selected for her first Commonwealth Games team. The second, a studio photo taken of Nina in her first campaign for the new range of L-EV8 sportswear. Hip, savvy and totally now.

The third was a photo taken without Nina's knowledge. Sitting in a late-night, take-away shop in the city. A half-finished burger and a few french fries lay on the table beside her camera. Nina had been caught at the moment she was putting the fries into her mouth. She had dark rings under her eyes, her face was puffy and pimply, and her hair lank.

There were more pictures inside. All of them unflattering. The photographer must have followed her around for a while. She wondered how he'd found her, if it were by chance or if he knew that her nocturnal meanderings were a regular thing.

The irony did not escape her. Exposed by the very piece of equipment she was hiding behind.

Nina walked out of the all-nite-mart and past the larger version of the magazine cover on a banner outside the shop.

'The tragedy of Nina Hallet, blown up life-size for everyone to see,' she said to herself.

179

It was Thursday night. Another night at the Bay Room. She didn't know if she would go now. Everyone would have seen the magazine. They would stare and whisper and smirk. Shan, Ruby and Sharon would sympathise, to her face, but Nina had no doubt they were enjoying her descent. It made them feel better about themselves.

What was a bit more embarrassment anyway? She'd lived with herself as the definition of failure for almost six months now. A few harmless sniggers were nothing to the way she could turn her mind inward and rip herself apart.

'The power of positive thinking,' she laughed bitterly to herself as she wandered along the esplanade. And anyway, a drink always helped.

But there was something more difficult to explain. Nina wondered if the photographer knew he had stolen one of the few comforts she had left.

Swimming had been her comfort once. The shortcomings she felt as a person were banished the moment she slipped into the water. With that gone, night time and her camera had become her solace.

She hated the photographer for taking that from her. Hated the magazine. Hated her swimming. She hated the world. There was one person to blame.

*

'I didn't mean it, Nina,' her mother declared. She got up from the chair she was sitting in when Nina walked through the door that afternoon.

Nina had found her mother sitting at the dining room table in tears. Sam was in the kitchen making tea. Her mother tried to give Nina a hug but Nina pushed her away.

'Did you have something to do with this?' Nina yelled at Sam, throwing the magazine down on the table.

'A woman from the magazine called to tell me she had

recent photos of you that the magazine was going to print and did I have any comment to make.' He spoke slowly as he poured the hot water into the teapot. When he had filled the pot he put the lid on and put it on a tray.

'Oh right, so how did they get quotes from Mum? Did you give them the number?' Nina couldn't stand the deliberate way Sam was going about the tea-making process.

'Nina, I am here to sit with your mother until your father gets home. In case you haven't noticed she's a little bit upset. I am not here to explain anything to you.'

There was no anger in his voice. He was just matter-of-fact as he brought the tray now laden with cups and saucers and sugar, over to the table.

Nina didn't know what to say. She stood there watching Sam set the table for her mother, all the while ignoring her. She was burning with accusations.

'I told the woman I didn't have anything to say,' her mother picked up the conversation. 'And she said that was okay. But then she told me she had these photos and they would write something anyway. She said "wouldn't it be better if I could write the truth". But I didn't realise it would be this . . .' her mother started crying again.

'Mum, that is such an old line! You should know that.'

'I just didn't want them to make it worse for you than it already is,' Nina's mother tried to explain but she could hardly speak through heaving sobs.

'You didn't care about me. You cared about you. Embarrassing pictures of your embarrassing daughter.'

'That's not true, Nina.'

Annette Hallet didn't feel like she had the strength to argue anymore. She put her face in her hands. All the months of worry poured out of her body. She blamed herself for everything that had happened to Nina. She was exhausted.

'All right, that's enough!' It was as if Sam had been given

the storm warning and had made a plan for the best way to survive it. He finished pouring her mother a cup of tea before going on. 'If you think your mother would deliberately do something to hurt you, then I feel sorry for you, Nina.'

'I don't need anyone to feel sorry for me,' Nina shot back. She was flustered. She hadn't expected to find Sam at the house. He and her mother had always disagreed on the way Nina should deal with the press. Now here he was at her mother's side. 'And you can't speak to me like this in my own home.'

'It's not your home. So either apologise to your mother or leave.'

'I beg your pardon!' Nina looked at her mother. Was she going to let him chastise her like that? But her mother didn't look at her. Sam went on, 'You're not the only person in the world to feel disappointment, Nina. It's the way people handle disappointment that determines whether they're champions or not. Winning has very little to do with it.'

Sam turned his back on her. She was dismissed. Her mother didn't look at her.

*

Nina sat squeezed amongst ten people around a small table in the Bay Room. Shan and Ruby were on one side of her, brazen and bold. But it was an act. None of this group would dare say or do anything unless the others sanctioned it, lest they be cast out, adrift in the land of thinking for yourself. Now Nina was one of them. She had never felt so alone.

Across the other side of the room Nicholas and Alice sat together with another group from school. Nina longed to go over there and just sit beside them. Not say anything. Just be with people who might try to understand everything that had been going on. They would probably even joke about it, send Nina up. Make her see the funny side of a world record holder slipping in the final at the Olympic games, instead of winning it. There had to be a funny side. Nina just couldn't see it yet. But there was no way she could go near them now.

'Hi Nina.'

Trent Hollingsworth squeezed himself in beside her. Trent had left school last year and gone to work immediately in his father's advertising company. He was popular. He was handsome. And he knew it. He had spent the last couple of weeks flirting with Nina. They had kissed on the dance floor a few times. But it hadn't gone any further than that. Nina was always pushing Trent's hands away. It wasn't that she didn't like his attention—every girl in Harper Bay wanted his attention. And his interest, for a moment, kept at a distance the voices that were on a permanent loop in her head. It's just that he was a bit full on.

She didn't really understand why he was interested in her. There were many girls who were more Trent's type. Perfectly made up, perfectly dressed girls. But he seemed to only have eyes for her.

As soon as he sat down his arm was around her shoulder, his hand on her chest where the layered tank tops she was wearing left it bare. Within moments his hand was gently stroking her skin and he was kissing her temples. As nervous as he made her, his touch was quite soothing after the dramas of the day. She drank the rest of her bourbon and coke and settled back in the chair.

'Here, you can finish my drink while I get us a couple more,' she heard him say. 'And then we should dance.'

They never made it to the dance floor. They were the only ones left in the booth by the end of the night. Nina had drunk more than she ever had. Trent had bought drinks for her all night. Said she should be spoiled. Told her how amazing she was. Told her that he wanted her all to himself. Kissed her. Amazing kisses. Like the ones she read about in the books of

Harriet Ray Walker. She let him touch her in places she had never been touched. In the dark shadows of the nightclub it seemed all the more thrilling.

'I could be so in love with you, Nina,' he said as the club was down to its last few occupants. 'Don't let me go home alone tonight,' he whispered.

'Come to my place,' she whispered back without really knowing what she was saying.

When she tried to stand she could hardly hold herself up. The room slid sideways as she grabbed the table to steady herself.

'Maybe this is not such a good idea.' The thought crossed her mind. She couldn't tell if she voiced it or not.

'Come on, princess, hold onto me,' and his arms were around her again. Steady arms, Nina thought.

A dark blur moved in from somewhere.

'Nina, do you want me to take you home?' She knew the voice. Felt a hand on her shoulder. Yes please, Nicholas, she wanted to say.

'Why would she want you to do that,' Trent spoke. There was a hardness in his voice she had not heard. 'Poofta,' he added.

The night air brought her speech back long enough to tell the cab driver her address. Trent's voice became more familiar in the back of the cab. He didn't stop talking as he smothered her. The movement of the car and Trent's heavy hands and body and mouth made it difficult to breathe. But she had never felt so wanted. Everything about her seemed to excite him. Nina was sure she would be excited too if she didn't feel so carsick. And wasn't so scared. From somewhere in her mind she heard, 'grow up, Nina, this is what being an adult is all about, it had to happen some time.' Resolved, she kissed him back. Hard.

'Oh, babe,' he responded.

Out of the cab, she stumbled again. He laughed. 'Drunk on the excitement of me, baby,' he said as he held her up again. She laughed too. A voice in her mind said, 'ugh'. She ignored it. She concentrated on getting them into her apartment.

She flicked on the light and headed straight for the fridge. She needed water. She stepped over all the stuff in her living room. Boxes that had never been unpacked. Clothes left where she'd taken them off. Overflowing ashtrays. Half empty glasses of soft drink. Pizza trays with leftovers from days ago.

She dragged the water jug from the otherwise empty fridge, supported her body by one elbow on the sink and rummaged through it for a semi-clean glass.

'Want some?' she asked Trent.

For a moment there was no reply. When his eyes met hers she saw the filth of the room reflected in them. For a moment she felt completely sober.

'No,' he finally answered.

She shrugged, poured water from the jug. Most of it landed in the sink. She chugged the water down her throat and dumped the glass back in the sink. She made her way back to where Trent stood in the middle of the room. His eyes had softened. Maybe he would understand.

'The last few months,' Nina tried to pronounce every word properly, 'have been a bit . . .' how could she describe it without telling him too much, '. . . weird.'

'Yeah, sure.' He pulled her into his chest. Started rubbing her back. It felt nice. His hand went under her clothes. Both hands against her skin. He leant down and started kissing her again. His hands played at her waist and suddenly they were pulling her tank top off. She wasn't sure that she was ready to be naked just yet. She resisted, kept her elbows down. But the moment she forgot, put her arms up around his neck to hold him, her top was off. In an instant they were on the floor. There were no words this time. Just Trent, insistent. Again she didn't know how to keep any control of his hands, his mouth and now his body, rubbing, pushing, feeling every centimetre of her. She couldn't breathe. She started to cry. Tried to tell him to get off.

Suddenly he was off her and on his knees. He did understand! She went to roll away. But as soon as his shirt was off he was on top of her again. Forcing her to touch him in places she didn't want to touch.

Her body shuddered. She knew it wasn't lust. She tried to tell him. Tried to push him off her so she could get to the bathroom. Or at least get him out of range. The searing bile forced its way into her throat. In an instant the contents of Nina's stomach were all over the both of them.

He yelped as he jumped away from her. Tried to wipe her vomit off his body, off his pants. At least she had got him off her.

'You revolting bitch,' he yelled. 'Ugh!' He crossed the floor on his way to the door with the kind of exaggerated step that said he could be contaminated at any moment.

'I came here to screw an Olympian and what did I get? A pig in a pigsty.' He spat at her. She felt it land on her stomach as she lay on the floor. 'You disgust me!'

The door slammed so hard it bounced back out of the lock. But Nina couldn't get up to close it. Or cover herself. The best she could do was roll over. She thought of her mum. How could you let yourself go like this?

Then she passed out.

*

Nina remembered arms helping her get off the floor. She remembered warm water trickling over her body and a soft flannel cleaning her up. She remembered sitting on the floor of the bedroom, wrapped in a towel, while her bed was made. Before she was allowed to slide into clean, crisp sheets she remembered her head being held, while she swallowed aspirin and drank a large glass of cold water. She tried to say sorry but a finger was put to her lips. 'Shhh' was the last thing she heard before she drifted off to sleep.

*

She sat at his feet, waiting for him to wake. He must have been up all night. Nothing about the apartment resembled the one that she had walked into a few hours earlier with Trent Hollingsworth. It was spotless. And smelt of disinfectant. The person who lived here before had been cleaned up and put away.

There was even a clean pair of cargoes and one of his T-shirts on the end of her bed when she woke up.

He must have fallen asleep, exhausted, in the old armchair. Except for the bed, it was the only piece of furniture she owned.

He had found her photographs. They were spread out on the floor around the chair. She looked at the photos. Her night people. Party people, homeless people, lovers, loners.

As she looked at them she realised the difference between the work she did and the work the photographer did for the magazine. She'd only ever looked through the lens to capture something in the world that was beautiful, or amazing, or something she never wanted to forget. Never to demean another person's experience. Suddenly she felt sorry for someone who had to lurk in the shadows looking for a moment like that.

'How's your head?' she heard Nicholas ask.

She kept her eyes down. She wanted to tell him about her discovery but she was too embarrassed to look at him. 'Not as bad as it might have been.'

He laughed softly. She smiled to herself. She didn't know where to begin. 'Don't know why you put up with me,' was the best she could do.

'No, me neither,' he said.

They sat for a moment without saying anything. It was the nicest moment Nina had felt for a long time. Nicholas broke the silence.

'Must be 'cause I miss my best friend.'

Nina didn't think she had ever heard sweeter words. She tried not to cry. He got down from the chair and sat next to her on the floor.

'Do you think I could have her back now, please?'

She nodded. How could she explain what had happened. 'Nicholas,' she did her best to speak. 'It all went so wrong!' She leant over and put her head on his chest.

'Oh, Nina,' he stroked her hair. Her body was overcome by wracking sobs that had been strangling her insides for too long. He waited until they subsided and then he spoke.

'I've got a couple of theories on this, if you want to hear them,' he said to the back of her head. He leant in and whispered, 'I think that what happened in Cape Town was a blessing in disguise.'

She sat up and wiped her face with the backs of her hands. She had no idea what he was talking about but she was willing to listen.

'What if you'd won? At sixteen you would have reached the pinnacle of human endeavour! Total achievement! The ultimate! What are you going to do with the rest of your life after that?' he asked her. 'Imagine what it would be like! You would have to tell the story over and over and over again, year after year, until, in about twenty years time you'd be saying to me, "Nicholas, I'm so bored! Doesn't anybody talk about anything else? I wish I'd never won those swimming races".'

He did such a perfect imitation of her she had to laugh even if the story seemed incredible.

'Then there would be all this other pressure. "What should I do Nicholas? How do I make the most of these gold medals I won? Should I keep swimming, should I do this, should I do that, when do I give up, what do I do after that?" Instead—no offence Nina—you've got a story no one really wants to hear.'

She winced at his words.

'No, I don't mean it like that. It's just not one of those gung-ho, what-a-winner, kind of stories.' He wasn't sure he was saying anything to make her feel better. 'What I'm saying is that you are totally free. You can look at all the things you are good at and take whichever path you want. There will be none of those "gee what a waste!" comments if you decide to go off and take photos of, I don't know, long-haired, killer Zacs in outer-Timbuktu, instead of being a sports commentator! And you'll have this big, wonderful, interesting life of which Cape Town was just one of many amazing moments.'

By the time he finished his speech his gesticulating had become so wild he almost lost his balance. He looked at Nina, eyebrows knitted, thinking about what he had said. He couldn't tell if she was totally convinced. Finally she ran her fingers through her hair which had dried in a mad frizz while she slept and her head started bobbing.

'So you're saying that if things had gone as I had hoped they would in Cape Town it would have been a disaster.'

'A catastrophe!'

She couldn't believe what she was going along with. 'A total tragedy.'

'An absolute nightmare,' he declared, exaggerating every syllable.

Nina didn't know if she was laughing or crying. 'That's some theory, Nicholas,' she finally managed to squeak.

'Well, I had a while to come up with it.' He was very serious now.

'Thank you.' It seemed too little to say when she felt so much.

With a big sigh, he reached over and took both her hands.

189

'I could have come up with it sooner, you know. All you had to do was ask.'

NINJA-NINA TAKES ON THE BIG APPLE
by Ron Samuels

After a year she would rather forget, teenage swimming favourite Nina Hallet is to take a break from the pool to pursue her other love, photography.

Speaking on the eve of her trip to New York, where she will work at the international headquarters of the popular young women's magazine *sAssy*, Hallet said she was looking forward to a career switch.

'It's something I have dreamed of doing since I first picked up a camera— ironically, as an assignment for *sAssy* on my first international tour as a swimmer. I've grown up, I've finished my HSC and I see the world in a different way these days. And this is the kind of opportunity that is too good to pass up. I just can't wait.'

Hallet would not be drawn on whether she would get back in the pool to avenge her disastrous experience at the Cape Town Olympics last year when she slipped in the final of the 200m Backstroke. She still holds world records for both the 100m and 200m Backstroke events.

'I don't feel I have anything to prove but you know what they say: "never say never". I just find myself drawn to different things these days. And the unknown is far more inspiring to me than a ride that I've already been on. But I'll let you know!'

CHAPTER TWENTY-ONE

'COMPLETELY SELF-INDULGENT if you ask me.' Nicholas took a bite from the apple and passed it to Alice.

'I bet it's only here because she's, like, an Olympian!' Alice took a bite of the apple. She stopped short of handing the apple on to Nina.

'Jealousy is such an ugly emotion!' Nina took the apple from Alice with a grin and took the biggest bite.

A car horn sounded. 'C'mon, we'll miss the plane,' Nicholas said, hitting Nina on the arm.

There was a convoy of cars heading to the airport to farewell Nina and Nicholas. They had parked illegally for a moment in order to look at the department store window.

Nina turned back around for a last look at her work, her Year 12 final project that had been chosen for this year's *FutureShock* art exhibition. It was a massive piece of collage, photomontage and mixed media, into which she had poured all the excitement, fear, frustration, failure and ultimately resolution of the last few years. At least, that was what one of the reviews had said.

It was in the main window of the city department store for everyone to see. Nina was pleased she had the chance to see it before she left for New York. She knew she had lived all the stuff that was up there but it felt strangely separate from her now.

'Nina,' her dad called from the car.

She checked to see there were no cars coming before she

ran across the road to join Alice in the back seat of her parents' car. Nicholas was travelling with his father in their car.

'What do you think?' her father said as she got in the car.

'I don't know, what do you think?' she said.

'I reckon it's great,' he said with a grin on his face as he pulled out from the curb.

Nina's mother swung around from the front passenger seat. 'Jake will be at the airport. He just called and he's leaving training now.'

Nina nodded. Jake had been the last to forgive her. She understood why. She understood a little bit about being in love and she knew she'd hurt him in ways she couldn't hurt the others.

'You guys are going to have the best time,' Alice broke in to Nina's thoughts. 'Is the magazine called *sAssy* over there too?'

Nina nodded. Tamasin had turned out to be an amazing friend. She had organised a three-month internship with *sAssy*'s sister magazine in New York. Tamasin had made it quite clear that she hoped Nina would bring her experience back and work for her again in Sydney.

When Nicholas agreed to go with her, Nina bought them both plane tickets that very day.

'You'll be needing this,' Alice pushed a very large package onto Nina's lap.

'Alice,' Nina protested. She tore off the wrapping and laughed. 'No,' Nina couldn't believe the present. 'This was for me?'

Alice's chubby cheeks wobbled as she giggled and nodded at the same time.

When Nina had gone back to finish Year 12 after her 'beige moment' as Nicholas called it, she had set about trying to make up with Alice. One day she had walked into class to find Shan prancing around in a brilliant red, chunky, cable knit

192

poncho. Nina had only seen pictures of sweaters like it in magazines. It was absolutely fantastic. But not very Shan.

'Get it off, Shan,' Nina heard Alice's voice from behind her.

'Hah,' Shan laughed. 'Where'd you pick up a gem like this, Alice? From your grandmother?' She got a laugh from a few in the classroom before she took it off and threw it at Alice.

'I will never understand you, Alice Hinkel,' Shan declared as she slid into the chair at her desk.

'That's because Alice is an original,' Nina retorted from her own seat. 'And that, Shan, is a word you'd have to look up.'

Nina remembered the smile on Alice's face. She held the poncho up in front of her. 'Look, Mum,' she called to the front seat even though she couldn't see her mother through the masses of red wool. 'Are you sure, Alice? It's just so cool!'

'Yeah, my grandmother did actually make it from a picture I showed her. So she can make me another one. You'll need it in the winter over there.'

Nina dropped the poncho and grabbed Alice's hand and squeezed it.

Nina laid her head back on the seat for the final few kilometres to the airport. Everything seemed perfect. She did a mental checklist. She was sure she'd remembered to do everything. She'd even managed to leave her mum and dad a card. It was sitting on the kitchen table, waiting for them when they got home from the airport.

Nina had taken a long time trying to decide which card to buy. In the end she went for a simple card with a little bit of colour. The only printed words were 'thinking of you'. She had taken even longer to decide what to write on the card. In the end, she had decided to keep it simple. 'Thanks for everything,' seemed to say it all.

Across the bottom of the card she had scrawled, 'All my love, Ninja'.

LISA FORREST is a TV and radio broadcaster, actor and writer. She lives in Sydney with her husband, Jesse, and their cat, Sugar Ray.

While she was never quite an international sports star, she did swim for Australia as a teenager. She competed at the 1980 Moscow Olympics and at the Commonwealth Games in Edmonton in 1978 and in Brisbane in 1982, where she won two gold medals.

This is her first novel.